The
Captive Sultan
and other stories

THE
Yom Tov
SERIES

The
Captive Sultan
and other stories

Adapted into English by
Avigail Teichman

CIS

C.I.S./Publications Division
Lakewood, New Jersey

Published by:
C.I.S./Publications Division
P.O.B. 26 Lakewood, N.J. 08701
Tel: (201)367-7858

Published in conjunction with:
Noam Shabbos Association
1569 Forty-Seventh Street
Brooklyn, N.Y. 11219
Tel: (718)438-6623

Typography:
C.I.S. Graphics
674 Eighth Street
Lakewood, N.J. 08701

Book Design:
Devorah Golshevsky

Book Production:
Malya Grunfeld
Sori Waxman

Printed and Bound by:
Gross Brothers, Inc.
Union City, N.J.

Contents

Publishers' Note

The Captive Sultan and other stories is the inaugural volume of *The Yom Tov Series* published by C.I.S./ Publications Division. This series features collections of inspiring stories relating to the special times of the Jewish year.

Through the pages of *The Captive Sultan and other stories* the reader will travel to the shores of Constantinople two centuries ago; plow through the snowdrifts of Poland and Russia; wander the midnight streets of Vilna with a simple peddler; visit a family in revolution-torn France; experience the chilling terror of Inquisition Spain; share the grief and the joy of a whole array of colorful characters. These stories are certain to touch and delight every member of the family.

Much of the credit for this book is due Rabbi Yaakov Kaluszyner of Noam Shabbos Association for his painstaking efforts in the selection of the stories. We also wish to express our thanks to *Yom Tov Ehrtzeilungen, Das Yiddishe Licht, Pardes Haggadah,* and Rabbi Tzvi Hirsch Myski for graciously granting us permission to adapt their stories for this volume. We would also like to note our appreciation to the talented and devoted members of the C.I.S graphics and editorial staff for a job well done.

The Captive Sultan

The Captive Sultan

IT WAS A LOVELY SPRING DAY in Constantinople. The sun was warm, the sky serene and blue. The lilacs were just coming out, perfuming the air with every breeze.

The streets of the city were crowded with people. In the marketplace merchants argued loudly with customers. Young apprentices were busy at the sides of carpenters, blacksmiths and masons. The shops were filled with talkative women and playing children. A buzz of activity was everywhere.

No one seemed to notice the tall broad-shouldered man

strolling across the square with long smooth strides. Although dressed as a peasant, he was decidedly a distinguished personage. The look of intelligence on his chiseled features and his aristocratic bearing belied the simple garb on his back. In fact, this was none other than the Sultan himself, who often disguised himself as an ordinary citizen and went out among his people.

The Sultan passed through the outskirts of the city undiscovered. Once along the open highway he threw back his head and laughed aloud. He was imagining the uproar he would have created had he been recognized in the square.

Now, the Sultan felt free to wander about as he pleased. He turned off the main road to explore a hidden path he discovered. Impulsively, he followed every curiosity that beckoned in the world of the forest. Here was a beaver dam, there an ant hill. Yonder were trees with exquisite blossoms and wild vines overhead beginning to bud. Deeper and deeper the Sultan lost himself in this great green wood.

The afternoon passed and the shadows of the trees grew long. The sun was distant and the air cool. The Sultan decided to return, but where was the original pathway? Here was only a narrow track that widened into a cobbled clearing. Beyond it grew a garden with trees concealing a brick wall. Who would choose to live secluded like this?

"Halt!" came a gruff command from behind. The Sultan barely had time to spin around before two robbers were upon him, searching his garments. A third ruffian stood by, keeping guard.

"Well, what have you found?" demanded the same voice.

"Nothing, nothing at all, Mechmet!"

"Hush!" cried the voice in great rage. "How dare you use my name in the presence of a stranger?"

Now the Sultan understood where he was. He had chanced upon the hiding place of the notorious bandit Mechmet and his henchmen.

"The peasant must die," continued Mechmet, "for he has

discovered us all."

The Sultan eyed the massive man before him, the long wild hair and the huge muscled arms.

"Speak!" commanded the bandit. "Now is your chance to utter your last words before your neck feels the edge of my knife."

Immediately, the Sultan fell to his knees, certain that he was about to die. He was on the verge of revealing his true identity and promising the bandit great rewards upon his safe return, but it occured to him that Mechmet might not believe him. Besides, even if Mechmet did believe him, he would probably not spare him. Once the Sultan was freed, he would surely send his royal army to capture Mechmet and his band. What guarantee would Mechmet have of his safety? Mechmet would surely not rely on just the Sultan's word.

"Well," thundered Mechmet. "What have you to say?"

"Perhaps," said the Sultan slowly, "I'd be worth more to you alive than dead."

"How so?"

"I've been taught a fine art which may bring you much profit," said the Sultan.

Mechmet showed little interest in this proposition, but with a weary wave of his hand, he bade the Sultan continue.

"My mother taught me to weave beautiful carpets with intricate designs. My work is far superior to that of others, and it commands a high price."

"Come," said Mechmet, intrigued in spite of himself. "I will keep you as a prisoner for three days. I will supply you with whatever materials you need, and you will weave in a small chamber undisturbed. Food and water will be left at your door. When you finish you will give your work to one of my men who will take it to market. If he returns by evening with the great price you say its worth, you may stay on and weave for me. If not, I will have the personal pleasure of separating your head from your neck."

And so it was. The materials were sent for and the

weaving begun. All the next day and far into the night the Sultan worked, thankful for the long disciplined hours he had spent learning carpet weaving at his mother's side. She had wanted to teach him the value of time, never allowing his hands to grow idle throughout the leisure hours at the palace, but little did she dream that someday her son's life would depend on this craft.

The Sultan's handiwork was indeed skillfully done. A brilliant pattern had been neatly designed into an exquisite carpet. Yet the true secret of his work would be revealed only to the most perceptive eyes. For the Sultan had secretly woven the first half of his royal insignia into the pattern. It could only be discerned when the carpet was held at a certain angle and studied closely under the light. But when examined just so, it was clearly, undeniably, the mark of the Sultan.

In the morning, Mechmet and Kumar, a trusted guard, appeared at the doorway of the chamber. The Sultan gave Kumar specific instructions.

"Take no less than five hundred dinars for this piece of work," he said. "A connoisseur will gladly pay this price for such a fine piece. The uneducated dealers will offer at most one hundred dinars, because they will not appreciate it. Do not let this discourage you. Take it everywhere until you get five hundred dinars."

The carpet was rolled up in a sack and tied onto the saddle of a big black horse. Kumar was already calculating his share of the profits as he rode swiftly on to Constantinople. Only when he reached the center of the city did he slow his gallop. He tethered the horse and pushed his way through the crowd until he came to the first stall.

"I have some good work to sell," he said to the stout man across the table.

"Well," said the man. "Let us see what you have."

Carefully, Kumar unrolled the carpet. It draped the long narrow table, bringing admiration from all sides. It was indeed an exceptional piece of art.

"How much do you want? Fifty dinars?"

"Bah!" scoffed Kumar.

"One hundred," said the merchant. "I'll take it for one hundred dinars."

The merchant mopped his brow and looked about at the people who had gathered. The spectators began to drift away, certain that the haggling had come to a conclusion. But Kumar's response drew them back again.

"Bah!" he shouted again. "You insult me! I'll take my merchandise elsewhere. To an artisan who truly knows his craft."

The stout man was embarrassed, his face crimson. Yet, he shrugged his shoulders for his pride burned within his chest.

"Ha!" he scoffed. "You won't find a better price elsewhere!"

Kumar ignored this remark and pressed further on until he found an old woman sitting behind linens working fine embroidery. Politely, he approached her and explained that he had an expensive carpet for sale. Perhaps she was interested. She agreed to take a look at it and make an offer.

"This," she said as she helped him spread it out, "is truly a masterpiece. You could easily get one hundred dinars for it. But if you try a little harder you'll make as much as as one hundred and fifty. As for me, I cannot afford more than seventy-five. Good luck."

She smiled and helped him roll the carpet neatly.

Kumar was undaunted. He continued seeking out weavers and linen dealers. At last he found five long tables covered with all sorts of splendid woven items. The merchants were gathered at one table, exchanging jokes and stories to pass the time until an interested customer would happen by.

Kumar drew near and waited until he caught the attention of one of them.

"What can I do for you?" asked the merchant.

"I see," Kumar replied loudly, "that this is a gathering of

connoisseurs. I myself have a unique piece. May I have the privilege of offering it?"

With great ceremony Kumar unrolled his carpet and held it high.

"Ah," came the exclamations from all around.

Kumar waited dramatically and said, "Well, do I have an offer?"

"One hudnred dinars," said a first.

"One hundred twenty-five," countered a second.

"One hundred thirty," shouted the first.

"One hundred forty-five," a third voice called.

"One hundred fifty," exclaimed the first.

Everyone fell silent. Again Kumar waited. He drew his breath and finally spoke.

"Do I hear more than one hundred and fifty dinars?"

No one moved.

"It's mine!" cried the first merchant. "I'll take it for one hundred and fifty. But what a high price to pay for so small a carpet. You've done well, sir. You know how to make a good profit."

He reached out to grasp Kumar's hand and finalize the sale, but Kumar withdrew it quickly.

"No," he said firmly. "I will not sell this piece for less than five hundred dinar."

All within hearing distance were stunned into silence.

"This cloth is for sale at five hundred dinars, not a dinar less." He repeated insistently. "Do I hear five hundred dinars?"

A ripple of laughter swept through the crowd and soon burst into a hilarious uproar. The people were pointing to Kumar and his carpet for sale at the ridiculous price of five hundred dinars. The crowd grew larger and the laughing louder. Kumar stuffed his carpet into its sack and dashed through the rocking mass. He searched the streets for a shelter, a place to conceal himself until the mockery subsided. Luckily, on the very next block was Levi's wine cellar.

Kumar stumbled down the narrow dark stairway into

the cool and dim room demanding a glass of water from the Jewish proprietor. Levi took one look at Kumar and ran off to bring him his glass of water.

"Where is everyone?" shouted Kumar, frenzied, surveying the deserted wine cellar.

"Haven't you heard? They've gone to see the spectacle."

"What spectacle?" Kumar asked, knowing full well the answer.

"They say there's a lunatic demanding five hundred dinars for a carpet."

Kumar made an effort to keep himself calm.

"Look at me," he said, "Look into my eyes. Do I look like a lunatic?"

"You?"

"Yes, me!"

"Certainly not!" said Levi shaking his head. "You look like an ambitious young fellow about his business."

"Well, so I am!" Kumar cried. "But for this accursed carpet. I've been commissioned to sell it for five hundred dinars, not a dinar less. And here I'm made the fool of the town."

"Will you let me see this extraordinary carpet?" Levi inquired. "I've learned weaving and would like to consider myself knowledgable in the art."

At first Kumar was hesitant. The insult he had just publicly endured was too fresh. He was unprepared for further ridicule. Levi understood his feelings and promised him to evaluate the masterpiece with the same respect that such merchandise deserved. This, and the memory of Mechmet and the prisoner's advice to persevere until the price was met, convinced Kumar to display the carpet once more.

He carefully unrolled it and spread it across the table. He waited for Levi to speak. Levi looked at it puzzled. Clearly, a young intelligent man stood before him. Yet he expected to be paid an outrageous price for the carpet. What could this mean?

Then it occurred to Levi that perhaps there was more to the design than met the eye superficially. Levi took the carpet to the doorway and examined it closely in the bright sunlight. Suddenly his eye caught the outline of the royal emblem. But this was only half of it. Abruptly, Levi looked up.

Kumar was watching at his side, unaware of the detection.

"Do you have any more carpets like this?" Levi asked quickly.

"In a few days I can bring another," Kumar replied with a smile as his face brightened, "That is, if you are willing to pay the price."

"Five hundred dinars?"

"Yes."

"If you wait a half hour, I'll have the sum sent for."

The bargain was struck and Levi put the carpet away.

Kumar was happy. His mission had finally been accomplished. Soon the workers returned to the wine cellar and resumed their tasks. They were laughing about the lunatic who demanded five hundred dinars for a piece of patchwork and then disappeared. Kumar nodded and laughed with them, enjoying the joke wholeheartedly.

Levi stood behind the counter tallying the sales and wondering about the court intrigue he had happened upon.

Word of the Sultan's absence had not yet gotten out. It was only the second evening he was gone and the royal family was unconcerned. It was not unusual for the Sultan to go on a mysterious excursion. But at court he was sorely missed. Important decisions were pushed off.

The Grand Vizier was under extreme pressure. All day long dignitaries and courtiers plagued him for his signature on edicts and petitions meant for the Sultan. Determined that something would have to be done, he set off to confer with the Sultana.

In the antechamber of the Sultana's sitting room, he was surprised to find Levi, a simple wine merchant anxiously awaiting an audience. The Grand Vizier could not help but wonder what urgent business this person might have with the Sultana.

After greeting him cordially, the Grand Vizier casually remarked, "It's quite late in the evening. The Sultana sees no one past the dinner hour."

Levi smiled nervously and nodded. Yes, this he knew.

"Then," continued the Grand Vizier, "I'm sure you won't be disappointed if you're turned away."

"Oh yes, yes I will," Levi said quickly.

"Well, how do you expect to gain an audience with Her Highness?"

"With the help of G-d, and the gracious messengers he sends," answered Levi modestly.

"Perhaps you regard me as one of those heaven sent angels," smiled the Grand Vizier. He was flattered and amused. It felt good to relieve some of the tension that weighed upon him all day.

Levi did not think this was a joke at all; he took the Grand Vizier's offer seriously. After all, the Grand Vizier had always been decent towards the Jewish citizenry. Maybe it would be wise to try and enlist the Grand Vizier's assistance. Levi bowed courteously and withdrew the rolled carpet from its sack. He offered it to the Grand Vizier.

"Does this mean anything to you?" he asked quietly. The Grand Vizier unrolled and examined the carpet.

"Nothing but the finest of gifts to present to her Royal Highness. I am an avid admirer of the woven arts."

"Is that all?" pressed Levi.

The Grand Vizier's brow furrowed as he studied the carpet closely, drawing it near to the lantern on the small corner table. "Aha!" cried he. "I have discovered the first half of the royal insignia woven into the pattern. How clever! Have you woven this yourself?"

"No," Levi was hesitant to continue. The Grand Vizier signaled him to speak. "I purchased it for five hundred dinars from a stranger. He told me that he could supply other samples of this artwork."

The Grand Vizier was instantly alert. Could this be a signal from the Sultan, perhaps lost or captured somewhere? Only the Sultana would know. Just then a page entered to usher him into her luxurious anteroom. The Grand Vizier pressed a coin into his hand and whispered something in the page's ear. The page then motioned Levi to follow with the carpet.

The Sultana received her guests most graciously. The Grand Vizier complained of the absence of the Sultan at court. The Sultana merely smiled and shrugged her shoulders. "He'll be back in the morning," she said. "And if not tomorrow, the next day. You'll see."

"Are you certain the Sultan is safe from harm? What do you think of this?" he signalled Levi to display the carpet.

The Sultana gasped, immediately recognizing her husband's handiwork. The Grand Vizier then brought the unfinished insignia to her attention. By now the Sultana was disturbed. At this juncture Levi told his story and begged the Sultana permission to purchase the next piece of work. If the second half of the emblem should appear on it, it was indeed a signal for help from the Sultan.

The Sultana sent for her treasurer and offered Levi one thousand dinars to include reimbursement for the first payment. But Levi refused to accept, explaining that he was glad G-d had given him the opportunity to prove his loyalty to the Sultan.

Levi returned the following evening to the palace. He brought with him the second purchase, another beautiful carpet with the second half of the insignia woven into the design. Now it was certain that the Sultan was being held captive somewhere.

The Sultana had her scribe make up a document granting Levi an immediate audience with Her Highness any time of the day or night. He was also given instructions to continue making these purchases until the Sultan was rescued. In the meantime, the courtiers were told that the Sultan had made a distant journey. Absolute secrecy was essential.

In the next carpet Kumar sold to Levi, the Sultan had spelled out the name of his captor. As he left the city, Kumar was followed discreetly by agents of the Grand Vizier. At last, the pathways leading to Mechmet's hideout were discovered.

Three days later a regiment of the royal army led by the Grand Vizier rode out on the highway. Rumors spread through the cobbled streets that they were going to greet the Sultan upon his expected return. The troops made their way through the forest until they came to the clearing the agents had described and surrounded the hideout.

The troops waited in perfect silence until the front door opened and Mechmet himself emerged, unaware. Immediately, four soldiers fell upon him and wrestled him to the ground. He called for help and instantly all ten of his henchmen appeared; only to be instantly overpowered.

Four more royal guards entered the hideout to unchain the Sultan and seek out the treasure.

Amid great cheers the Sultan rode home through the streets of Constantinople. Chained together, Mechmet and his bandits followed behind him. The Grand Vizier and his troops rode alongside. It appeared to the townsfolk that their beloved Sultan had secretly gone to capture the dreaded Mechmet and once again returned as the victorious hero.

By the time the Sultan reached the palace gates a huge parade followed. The Sultana came out to greet him.

They had a hundred things to say to each other. The Sultana's eyes were filled with joyous tears. She was bursting with expressions of gladness for him. But the Sultan pressed his finger to his lips.

"We will speak later," he said gently. "First tell me who has been buying my carpets. I must reward him."

The Sultana clapped her hands and Levi appeared from the next room, bowing politely.

"I owe my life to you," said the Sultan. "What is your

name, my good friend?"

"It was G-d that saved the Sultan, not I. I am Levi, the wine merchant. I am only an instrument employed by G-d."

"You speak humbly," replied the Sultan. "Of course, we must thank G-d, but you do deserve some reward."

"My reward has been to see the Sultan alive and well."

"Very well then," said the Sultan with a wave of his hand. "I have no time for petty modesty. Go home and return any time of the day or night to make your request."

The Sultan called for his scribe and issued a second letter of admission for a royal audience at any time, open to any of the members of Levi's immediate family.

Levi thanked the Sultan profusely. The Sultan dismissed him shortly and Levi bowed out. He carefully placed the royal document in his saddle bag.

All his life Levi treasured this precious letter, but he never made use of it. He truly saw himself as a simple Jew, privileged to assist the mighty Sultan. If he had requested a reward he would certainly have received it, but he would have been soon forgotten. Now, he had the opportunity of displaying his unselfish loyalty as a Jewish citizen by refusing reward. How well this would speak of his people at court!

As time moved on the letter was carefully passed on to Levi's eldest son as a page in the history of the family legacy.

During this time, too, the Sultan died and the crown was passed on to his eldest son. Much like his father, he enjoyed going out among his people to breathe in the first breath of spring.

The young Sultan rode on horseback accompanied by a favorite advisor, Salada. As they galloped leisurely out of the city and along the highway, they passed a wagon loaded with sacks of flour. Overlooking the bundles sat a Jewish man with a long white beard and earlocks. Another Jewish man with a black beard drove the wagon.

"What's this?" asked the Sultan. He was eager to learn about the various occupations of his subjects.

Salada shrugged his shoulders as if unconcerned.

"Just some simple old Jews," he replied indifferently. "Hardly worthy of Your Majesty's attention."

"But, I want to know about all my subjects," insisted the Sultan. "Regardless of status or race. Are you not kindly disposed to all my citizens?"

Salada felt the Sultan's growing suspicions of his impure motives and hastily smiled.

"I'm sorry that I have not been sensitive to your curiosity. If you wish to understand all the religions in our land, I shall do the best I can to tell you about the Jews."

Salada paused and then suddenly his face brightened with wicked pleasure.

"The Hebrew holiday of Pesach (Passover) begins in three days," he said. "In commemoration of their exodus from a heathen land, the Jews mix flour with blood to make a dough that is baked. This flat unleavened bread is called matzoh. Eating this blood-baked matzoh is the main feature of the Holiday."

Salada spoke quickly and clearly. Now he sat back and waited for the Sultan to speak.

"I never heard of baking with blood in any religion. Before today that is. What type of blood do the Jews use?" he asked.

Salada did not reply.

"Well," the Sultan said impatiently, "don't you know?"

"Yes." Salada feigned hesitance. "I do know. But this is the very reason that I have tried to avoid the subject in the first place. It pains me to speak of the matter, and it will disturb Your Majesty no less."

"Speak!" commanded the Sultan, his curiosity greatly aroused.

"The blood of a Moslem child!"

Salada's words were shrill and sharp. He let a heavy silence follow as their meaning penetrated the Sultan's mind.

The Sultan was sickened and stopped his horse.

"I can't believe such a thing," he spluttered. "My father always thought well of the Jews. Why has no one ever done anything about this?"

Salada was quick to reply.

"The Jews are shrewd people," he said. "They do their work with the utmost secrecy and take every precaution. Each step of their procedures is codified with exact details. The entire process is observed and guarded by special watchers. There is no religious practice so highly scrutinized in this or any other religion. When I was studying about the different beliefs around the world I read about this dreadful Jewish custom in an ancient history book."

The Sultan was overwhelmed.

"Can you prove this to be true?" he asked, already half convinced.

"Perhaps we can turn around and overtake that suspicious wagon. Question the Jews yourself. You'll see that their replies will coincide with my allegations."

Within a few minutes they overtook the strange wagon. The Sultan stopped the driver and questioned him. The Jew admitted that the flour was for the baking of matzos eaten on the Holiday and that the procedure involved was followed with great care. All that he said verified Salada's words except that he made no mention of blood. Instead, he explained that water was used for the dough.

"Of course," said Salada, when they rode away, "the Jew will not divulge the infamous secret of the crime."

The Sultan rode in thoughtful silence for a long while. The picturesque roadside meant little to him now.

"Can I allow such a cruelty to go unpunished in my province now that I have been made aware of it?" he mused aloud. "What shall I do?"

"Perhaps I can make a suggestion," Salada offered.

"Speak!"

"On the first night of the Holiday have ten Jewish homes spied upon throughout their feast. The spies will establish that the Jews do indeed make the matzoh an integral part of the evening. The next morning the entire Jewish populace will be gathered in the synagogue. There you can announce your decree of justice."

The Sultan was relieved and thanked Salada for his advice. Yes, he would follow this fair plan of action, the Sultan reflected. Salada had eased his mind.

Though he rejoiced greatly in his heart, Salada wisely spoke no more of the matter. His plot was perfect. He wanted no one to interfere.

"Perhaps we should keep this confidential," he said to the Sultan before they reentered the city.

The Sultan nodded in agreement, and already pretending, he asked in mock perplexity, "My dear Salada, what under heaven do you speak of?"

Salada was now reassured. The conspiracy was foolproof.

That night Salada slept peacefully. But on the other side of the village Eliezer ben Levi awoke with a shiver. In the midst of his sleep, the face of his long departed father appeared. It so startled Eliezer that he sat bolt upright in bed. After a few moments, he calmed himself enough to lie down. Then again, as he began to doze, he heard his father's voice calling and the image reappeared.

"Don't be frightened," he heard a dreamlike voice say. "It is I, Levi ben Yitzchok, your father."

Eliezer contained himself as his fear slowly gave way to a boyish longing. He listened and watched with burning intensity.

"I have been granted permission from the Merciful G-d to communicate with you. It is up to you to avert the impending disaster, the Sultan's decree, to be announced the first morning of Pesach. Go find my letter of royal visitation privileges and bring it to the Sultan immediately. Do you hear me? Do you hear me?"

At this point, Eliezer awoke, greatly confused. He got out of his bed and washed his hands. He paced the bedroom floor, by now fully awake and frightened. He knew he could not sleep in this state of frenzy.

Eliezer went into the study and lit his lantern. He found his *Tehillim* and began to recite, page by page. How soothing were the ancient verses, the consolation of his people for thousands of years, in the stillness of countless nights. Eliezer calmed down sufficiently to finish learning a piece of *G'mara* he had started earlier that day. He became so engrossed in a difficult passage that he soon lost himself completely in the intricacies of his study.

So the night passed, and by dawn the dream was no more than an unsettling memory. At first Eliezer thought he'd ask the *Rav* what it meant. But on second thought, it might have been just an ordinary illusion. Besides, there was no time. There were so many other things to do today. Tonight would be *Bedikas Chometz*. He'd have to sell his whiskey and give his wife some help with the *kashering* of the kitchen utensils.

It was very late that evening when Eliezer wearily climbed into bed. The day had been full, and he had hardly slept the night before. Sheer exhaustion soon led to deep slumber.

Again Levi's face appeared. He admonished his son for taking no action all day. Now Levi begged him to obey upon awakening. He should take the royal document and demand an audience with the Sultan. The fate of the entire Jewish community lay in his hands.

Eliezer awoke. The dream had been so real. Perhaps he should go and find that document this very minute. He got up and went into the study. He lit the lantern and opened his desk, scanning each drawer.

His wife was awakened by the flickering light and the shuffling sounds. What was he up to at this late hour? she wanted to know. Didn't he realize that there was so much to do tomorrow, and a good night's sleep was essential for both of them?

Eliezer tried to explain what he was doing, but it sounded so ridiculous and far-fetched that he didn't even bother. After all, his wife was right. He did have many responsibilities tomorrow, too many to risk for a dream that probably didn't mean anything anyway. He gave up his search for the document and went back to bed.

So *Yom Tov* came and Eliezer and his wife were prepared for the *Seder*. The guests arrived and the children were filled with anticipation. There was *kiddush, Mah Nishtanah, matzoh,* wine and *marror.* No one noticed the Sultan's spy that stood concealed behind a bush, looking into the window. Far into the night, the family and guests sat and discussed the *Hagaddah.* Finally, they concluded the *Seder* with the traditional songs of praise. After attending to the needs of his guests, Eliezer went to sleep.

Once again his father appeared to him in his dream, but this time he appeared greatly shaken. Speaking with urgency, he bade his son to act before it would be too late.

"Go," he said. "See the Sultan now. Tell him that the *matzoh* you eat is made of water and flour. Tell him that the informer who has told him otherwise is an impostor seeking power. In his bedroom are the strange idols he worships. He only pretends to be Moslem. Go, my son, immediately, before the Sultan's decree is executed."

Instantly, Eliezer arose and dressed. After a short search, he found the document in the bottom of his desk. Stealthily, he left the house and quickly walked out into the dark street. He looked heavenward and uttered a prayer for G-d's assistance on this *Lael Shimurim* — Night of Heavenly Watch.

In a half hour, Eliezer reached the palace gates. The guard refused to admit him at this late hour. Eliezer showed him the letter, and the guard took it inside. Shortly, he returned and allowed Eliezer to pass. The next guards let him pass unquestioned, already aware of the document he possessed. But when Eliezer asked for an audience with the Sultan he was firmly refused. No one could wake His Majesty at this hour with or without authentic privileges.

"At least," pleaded Eliezer, "could I see the Sultan's

mother? She will remember my father, Levi the wine merchant, and receive me well at any hour. I have come for an emergency."

This the page consented to do, and soon Eliezer was invited into the Sultana's luxurious anteroom.

"I hope I haven't disturbed your sleep," Eliezer apologized politely, "but I have come on an urgent matter."

"I don't sleep much anyway," the elderly Sultana said with a smile. "I'm thankful for any visitors at this lonely hour. Now what is your business?"

"I hesitate to speak because you may doubt me," Eliezer said slowly. "But perhaps the memory of my good father will help you believe my word."

"Yes, I remember your father well. He was a loyal admirer of my husband who refused any reward for saving his life. Perhaps here is the opportunity for me to repay him now, through you."

"If you will believe what I have to say and convince the Sultan of its truth you will have rewarded us all far more than we merit."

"Speak!" commanded the Sultana.

Eliezer then related his dream of three consecutive nights and the impending disaster they implied. He spoke of the impostor Salada and his secret idolatry. The Sultana listened patiently.

"I'll do what I can," she told Eliezer when he finished.

The Sultana was the only one able to awaken her son the Sultan. She went to his room and gently sat at the foot of his bed.

"My son," she said softly. "Arise. It is I, your mother."

"What is it?" cried the Sultan sitting up suddenly.

"Your father has just appeared to me in a dream, and I cannot have peace till I discuss it with you."

"Mother," said the Sultan, "perhaps you only imagine that you heard my father. I know it is difficult for you to sleep and how you long for his company."

"There is an unscrupulous advisor in your court who

only pretends to be Moslem. He has won your favor and plans to take advantage of your friendly disposition toward him for his own selfish motives. Already he has plotted an evil conspiracy which you have innocently approved. If you follow his malicious designs G-d will punish you and curse our great name. Your father has bade me to confront you this very minute, to sever your association with this heretic and spare us the consequences he may bring upon us all."

"I do not understand —"

"Have you made any decrees which will be acted upon tomorrow?" the Sultana asked quickly.

The Sultan thought for a moment and said, "Yes. As a matter of fact, I have. But there is no one that is aware of its contents save I and my faithful advisor Salada. How is it possible for you to have known?"

The Sultan sat silently for a moment, beginning to feel uneasy.

"What proof is there of Salada's heresy?" he asked.

"This too your father has revealed to me. In his private bedroom are hidden all sorts of idols he worships. Discover the truth for yourself. Send your guards to search his home right now, when he is not forewarned."

The Sultana's advice was good, and the Sultan accepted it. Immediately, he dispatched six guards with royal warrants to Salada's home to search his private bedroom. Salada was to be arrested and brought to the palace if evidence of secret idolatry were found.

Only then did the Sultana return to Eliezer, who was anxiously awaiting her. She told him how she had changed his story to make the facts more believable to her son. In a short while, they were interrupted by a knock at the door to her waiting room. It was the Sultan himself.

"Quick," the Sultana said to Eliezer. "Hide in my closet until I ask you to come out."

The Sultan's face was ashen. His guards had already returned with sufficient evidence of Salada's heresy. All that his mother said must be true. Salada himself was imprisoned in the castle dungeon to await sentencing.

How close the Sultan had come to betrayal of all the moral values of justice that made him worthy of rulership! The Sultan fell to his knees and thanked his mother.

"It is the true G-d in heaven whom you must thank," she said. "He has revealed the truth for your benefit in a dream through your beloved father. Now it is your responsibility to nullify the decree you have made under wicked influence."

The Sultan arose. "Yes, mother, you are right. Now, how shall I deal with Salada?"

"That is up to you, my son. You are the one who has been betrayed. Get some rest now and you'll decide in the morning when your head is clear. Enough has been accomplished tonight."

The Sultan thanked his mother again and bid her good night. When the Sultana heard his footsteps fade away down the hallway, she called for Eliezer to come out of hiding.

"Have you heard our conversation?"

"Yes."

"Are you satisfied?" asked the Sultana, smiling.

"Far more than I imagined possible," Eliezer replied. "I hardly know what words could adequately describe my gratitude and appreciation to you for saving so many lives and —"

"Remember," interrupted the Sultana. "This is my way of thanking your father. It was he who saved the life of my husband, which was worth more to me than all the lives in Constantinople."

Eliezer bowed.

"It is as you yourself have said to the Sultan. These are the wondrous workings of the All-Merciful G-d. Down through the ages, every first Passover night, He protects His Jewish children from harm in all sorts of miraculous ways."

A Protected Night

A Protected Night

IT WAS *EREV PESACH* in the little ghetto of Chantieres during the time of the French Revolution. France was in chaos, ravaged by marauding bands of peasants, but in Chantieres the main source of excitement was the imminent arrival of *Pesach*. The people scurried about on last minute errands, everyone involved with his own task. Suddenly, a wagon came hurtling through the streets, its driver shouting at the top of his lungs. It was Yossel the Wagon Driver urging all the people to stop and gather around to hear the important news he had brought.

"I've been on the road for four days," he shouted when a sizeable crowd had assembled. "I've ridden at great speed to come home before *Yom Tov*. I expected to be here early this morning, but I was accosted along the way."

Yossel stopped a moment to catch his breath while a murmur of dread spread through his listeners.

"But as you can see," he continued, "*Baruch Hashem* I've been spared and my wagon is still intact. It is a heavenly miracle that I stand here before you. Perhaps Hashem has spared my life and my vehicle so that I may bring you this warning."

The people stood still, hanging on Yossel's every word.

"A band of two hundred peasants led by two powerful ruffians overtook me. I was certain I was doomed, and I had already said *Sh'ma* when one of the leaders ordered me to halt. I did so immediately and resigned myself to my fate. However, the second leader merely asked about the contents of my cargo. I told him it was wine. He approached, slapped his great arm on my back and, smacking his lips, ordered me down from my seat. I obeyed. He turned his head for a moment, and I quickly fled into a thicket of trees by the roadside. I climbed into a giant oak and continued to watch from afar. Some of the men complained of the ease of my escape and wanted to pursue me. They would rather have ripped my flesh from my bones.

"'Don't worry,' their leader calmed them. 'There are many more like him in the village ahead. We'll plunder it next. Let us now savor his Passover wine.'

"At his signal, the band jumped onto the wagon, rocking it to and fro. They tore off every barrel. First the leaders were given to drink and then all the men fought over the wine like animals. In this way, they rioted until the last barrel was overturned, kicked open and emptied. Soon afterwards, they all left, singing and laughing in hilarious drunkenness as they slowly moved down the road.

"I waited until I could hear them no more. I thanked Hashem for sparing my life and emerged from my hiding place. My horse had waited patiently throughout the ruckus and my wagon, as you see, also survived the attack. I took a different road to avoid the band and rode faster than I have in years. The band will probably be here in about three hours."

Everyone began to speak at once making a great commotion. Where should they hide? What of their property? Soon it would be *Yom Tov. . .*

A tall commanding personage stepped up onto the wagon next to Yossel. Everyone recognized Reb Ber, the richest Jew of the town. He owned the great house next to the bridge at the edge of the village. People liked and trusted him, and now they quieted to hear what he had to say.

"Rabbosai," he called out as he turned to the left and the right, catching everybody's eye. "I suggest you continue your *Yom Tov* preparations as usual. But when you get home wrap up and hide all your valuables, including your jewelry and silver. No *Yom Tov* candles should be lit. Go to *shul* to *daven Minchah* and *Maariv,* but do not return home for the *Seder.* I want you all to fetch your wives and children and bring them to my house. We will all hide in my great basement until the danger has passed and the wild band has come and gone. Then you can go back home, light the candles, and make your *Sedarim."*

No one protested, and the plan was adopted. Three brave watchmen were set up at various checkpoints to signal the approach of the marauders. *Yom Tov* came, and the full white moon stood out in the black velvet sky. The ghetto was dark and quiet except for one little cottage that stood on the other side of the bridge, just outside the ghetto.

The *Yom Tov* candles danced and shone on the *Seder* table. Expensive silver and china bedecked each place set with white linen napkins and crystal goblets. These were the glorious treasures of Yankel the Butcher, bought from his meager earnings in honor of *Pesach.*

One of the watchmen reported this breach in strategy to Reb Ber.

"Go warn him," Reb Ber commanded, "that he'll ruin us all with those *Yom Tov* candles. Tell him to save himself and his family in the security of my basement. He should do no different from the rest of us!"

The watchman ran to Yankel's house and informed him of the impending disaster.

"I know, I know," replied Yankel with a shrug. "Don't you think I've been to *shul*? Now please let me continue the *Seder*. My youngest son was about to say the *Mah Nishtanah*. Perhaps you'd like to stay and hear?"

"You don't understand!" insisted the watchman. "You're making yourself a sure target for those madmen! Once they find you with all of your valuables, they won't stop searching until they've found all of us."

"Are you really afraid on this *Lail Shimurim*, Mr. Watchman?" said Yankel, growing red with anger. "Don't you think Hashem can look out for His people without your help?"

"Of course, of course," the man replied somewhat embarrassed. "But we can't rely completely on miracles, we must put in some effort ourselves."

"Just as the Jews of *Mitzrayim* were told to make a *Seder* to protect themselves *Pesach* night, so will I." Yankel's eyes were ablaze. "This is my effort. If you do not care to join us in this *mitzvah* you may go. *Gut Yom Tov.*"

Yankel returned to the table in his white *kittel*. The watchman shrugged his shoulders, sighed and left. He understood there was nothing more he could do. When he had gone, Yankel's wife and children looked at him beseechingly. Perhaps the watchman was right. If the entire *Kehillah* was hiding out, was it right to separate themselves?

"Where's your *bitachon*?" Yankel asked softly. "Come my children, tell me what you've learned about Hashem's wondrous ways and His faithful protection."

They went through the *Haggadah* in undisturbed discussion and holy joy. So absorbing was the *Seder* that no one around the table noticed the two vulgar faces staring through the window as they sang *Hallel.*

The band had arrived, just coming off the highway, and this was the first cottage they had come upon. Their leaders had told them to wait quietly until given the signal to attack. The rest of the populace shouldn't be aroused or alarmed by any unnecessary noise.

The first leader was greatly impressed with what he witnessed as he pressed his nose to the window. Never before had he seen such supreme glory on the faces of simple folk. The melody the children sang with their father was as beautiful as it was uplifting. The father dressed in white and the table set with silver — surely he was gazing upon an angelic scene. These were not ordinary people. They were heavenly beings.

The second leader, however, was more impressed with the booty that would soon be theirs.

"Let's go!" he whispered to his comrade.

"Sh!" said the other. "Let me look a while longer."

"But what are you waiting for?" the second leader grumbled impatiently, biting his lip and stamping his feet.

After a few moments the first leader spoke.

"Let us leave this home in peace," he said. "Indeed, let us leave this entire town in peace. There are plenty of other towns for us to plunder."

"But what of all the loot?" protested the other.

"If you say another word about this place I'll bash your head with my mallet this very minute!" threatened the first leader, squaring his shoulders. He was in fact much stronger than the other, and as such, he was first in command.

In the meantime, the marauders were growing restless.

"Go tell the men," said the first leader to the second, "that we will leave this cottage, which isn't worth a *sou*, for better profits elsewhere."

The band turned about and headed for the main high-way, leaving the ghetto in peace.

All this time, the three watchmen stood in their posts

transfixed by fear. As soon as the marauders left, the watchmen ran to Reb Ber's home to relate what they had seen.

"*Baruch Hashem*, the danger has passed," announced Reb Ber. "We all owe our lives to Reb Yankel the Butcher. It is he who has done properly by leading the *Seder* and placing his faith in Hashem. It is in his merit that Hashem took mercy and spared us all. Let us go to his house and tell him so."

Reb Yankel's wife Sarah had just been clearing the table when she heard a great crowd surrounding the house.

"Yankel, come quickly!" she cried. "I fear the attackers have arrived! *Oy*, what shall we do? Where shall we hide?"

Just then the door burst open and the familiar faces of friends and relatives appeared.

"*Gut Yom Tov, gut Yom Tov!*" the people called with smiles.

"Ah!" said Yankel his face lighting up with happiness. "So you've decided to come join me for the *Seder*. Come Sarah, let us make room. . ."

The Midnight Visitor

The Midnight Visitor

REB ZAIDEL OWNED a little teahouse and roadside inn just outside Bialystok. The Jewish travellers coming off the main road appreciated Reb Zaidel's personal service and friendly accommodations. His wife Henya was a wonderful cook who always had ample food warming on the stove.

The day before *Erev Pesach* arrived, and there was still much shopping to do. Reb Zaidel left his wife in charge of the kitchen and set off to Bialystok early in the morning.

It was almost dark when Reb Zaidel returned. His cart

was loaded with the bundles and packages he had purchased for *Yom Tov*. Reb Zaidel felt he had accomplished a
great deal, for among the regular purchases lay a small box
wrapped in colorful paper. In it was an exquisite golden
kiddush cup. Reb Zaidel had hardly expected to find such a
special piece with which to adorn his *Seder* table this year.

He tied his horse to the post outside the teahouse and
ran inside.

"Henya, Henya!" he shouted full of excitement.

"What is it? What is it?" she called running into the
hallway wearing her apron and wiping her wet hands on a
towel. "Why all this tumult? Don't you know we have guests
in the inn? You will disturb them."

Reb Zaidel had been so preoccupied with his prized
acquisition he hadn't noticed the other horses tethered
outside. Instantly, he put away the box and followed his
wife into the dining room.

"*Shalom Aleichem*! Welcome!" he called out to his guests.
"What an honor it is to have you here with us!"

He shook each visitor's hand heartily, introducing himself and learning their names.

"I apologize for making such a rude entrance," he said to
them. "I was just so excited at my good fortune I couldn't
control myself."

"May we share your good *mazel* with you?" the one
named Reb Hershel inquired. "Can you tell us about it?"

"Yes, yes, of course!" Reb Zaidel beamed. "But I must have
my wife here, too. She is such a diligent woman she wastes
no time and has already returned to her stove. Henya,
Henya, please come and see!" he called out once again.

When Henya returned to the dining room, the guests
stood up and crowded around while Reb Zaidel held the
unopened box in his hands.

"Every *Pesach* we adorn our *Seder* table with a new item
in honor of *Yom Tov*," he explained. "In past years, I have
bought expensive linens, china, crystal and silver, which we
reserve exclusively for use on *Pesach*. But this year we

couldn't find anything we didn't already have. I searched the tables in every stall in the marketplace today. A *matzoh* cover? A *Seder* plate? A pillow cover? We had them all.

"It was growing quite late, and I thought I'd have to return home emptyhanded. Just then, my eyes caught the rays of the sinking sun reflected on a bright piece of metal on a table I had somehow managed to overlook. I moved closer to this table, and behind some tin cups I found this precious golden goblet. Just perfect for Eliyahu Hanavi!"

With this Reb Zaidel carefully opened the box, withdrew the gold cup and unwound the protective cloth wrapped around it.

Henya clapped her hands with delight and a murmur of admiration filled the room. Each guest felt the thrill of handling this expensive piece, a piece truly fit for a king.

"But why do you wish to make this *mitzvah* on *Pesach* so special above all others?" asked the one named Sheftel, a strong note of resentment in his voice. "After all, do we have the right to spend such great amounts on ourselves when we can give it to *tzedakah* for others?"

Reb Zaidel did not seem to notice Sheftel's deep personal bitterness. He simply sighed to himself. Henya's eyes were downcast. Finally, Reb Zaidel answered.

"*Baruch Hashem*, I've been blessed with many good things. A wonderful wife, a good livelihood and true friends. Yet several years have already passed since we were married and we still have no children. Perhaps in the merit of beautifying this particular *mitzvah* of *Pesach*, Hashem will answer our prayers. After all, our matriarch Sarah was promised the birth of our patriarch Yitzchak when the angels came to visit on *Pesach*. If Eliyahu Hanavi is to come bring us Hashem's blessings for children isn't it more likely to happen on the *Seder* night than on another night?"

The guests listened to Reb Zaidel with sympathetic expressions on their faces.

"And now with this *kiddush* cup," he concluded, "Eliyahu Hanavi is certain to feel welcome in our humble home!"

Everyone laughed and cheered Reb Zaidel's good intentions, wishing the good couple much *mazel.*

Pesach night came, and the air was filled with a special holiness. Reb Zaidel returned from *shul* to find his wife waiting for him in their private cottage behind the inn. The lovely *Seder* table was laid with the finest pieces shining brilliantly in the light of the *Yom Tov* candles. The white linen cloth matched Reb Zaidel's *kittel.* His wife had sewn them both from the same expensive fabric. There was even an *afikomen* bag to match. It lay beside the three *shmurah matzos,* hidden under their embroidered white cover. The *Seder* plate was already colorfully arranged. The deep purple wine glistened in the crystal decanter on the other side of the table. Amidst all this splendor stood Eliyahu's golden goblet in supreme elegance.

Observing all this, Reb Zaidel felt like a king. He made *kiddush,* chanting each word with fervor. He discussed the *Haggadah* with Henya. Later he said *Hamotzi* with all the joy the *matzos* of freedom could bring.

They had just begun their *seudah* when Reb Zaidel confided the reason for his high spirits to Henya. Somehow he felt sure that this year they would merit Eliyahu Hanavi's company. Just at this point, they were startled to hear a knock at the door. Henya went to open it.

A tall man with an exceptionally long white beard entered. Without speaking a word, he made his way through the hallway and sat down at the *Seder* table. He was hardly dressed for *Yom Tov* in his rough workshirt and wide belt. Still, he seemed very purposeful and fully aware of what was going on.

"*Gut Yom Tov,*" said Henya timidly. "Can I serve you something?"

The stranger nodded and Henya went off to the kitchen.

"*Gut Yom Tov!*" said Reb Zaidel, offering his hand to the visitor. The man took his hand but did not reply. He looked the other way. This was no ordinary beggar, thought Reb Zaidel. Perhaps it is Eliyahu Hanavi himself, he thought with rising excitement. Perhaps it is beneath him to speak with a simple owner of a teahouse.

Henya returned carrying a tray laden with all sorts of special dishes. Reb Zaidel watched his guest closely, curious to see what he would do with the food set before him. Would he burn it up as did the angels who had come to visit Avraham? Reb Zaidel was surprised to see this man devour every delicacy like any hungry beggar. Reb Zaidel did not know what to make of his guest. Baffled, he said nothing. Henya, taking her cue from her husband and the stranger himself, made no conversation. They all ate in silence.

Reb Zaidel's wonder grew as he finished the meal and drank the third cup of wine. He still had no clue to the identity of his guest. Soon the gleaming golden goblet was filled for Eliyahu. Suddenly, Reb Zaidel had an idea. By offering the stranger to drink of it, he'd test his reaction and determine just who he really was.

The guest gravely nodded his agreement to drink from the cup. Now Reb Zaidel was certain he was sitting in the presence of Eliyahu Hanavi. The stranger drank some of the wine, fingered the goblet as he looked it over and smiled.

He's pleased, thought Reb Zaidel proudly. Henya too was happy.

The man withdrew a tiny silver box from his chest pocket. He opened it and sprinkled some of its black powder into the remaining wine in the goblet. He motioned for Reb Zaidel and his wife to drink it.

Surely, this must be a special potion for the blessing for children, thought Reb Zaidel. He eagerly drank from the cup and then offered it Henya.

"No, thank you," she murmured uneasily. "Did you forget wine is too strong for me? I only drink grape juice."

The stranger frowned at this and waved his hand indicating this was nonsense. Reb Zaidel urged his wife to drink. Henya gave in and with a shiver gulped down the remaining ounce.

Within moments, Reb Zaidel and Henya began to feel

drowsy. Reb Zaidel leaned back on the pillow in his chair and Henya begged to be excused so she could lie down on the couch. Soon both husband and wife were sleeping deeply.

Only the stranger remained fully conscious. He opened his shirt and a neatly folded black sack tumbled out. Quickly he began to stuff the expensive tableware and decorative pieces into his sack. The table was halfway cleared when he was disturbed by a second intruder.

"What are you doing?" the second intruder shouted hitting the first stranger with his cane. At this moment, the stranger was just picking up the beautiful golden goblet, and his long beard became entangled in its ornate stem. He jerked his shoulders back from the blow. His long white beard came away and was left hanging from the goblet.

"I'm lost!" he shrieked.

His cry awoke Henya who looked about, confused. A shocking sight met her eyes. The *Seder* table was half cleared, and nearby was a black sack half filled with her silver. And who were these two strangers locked in angry confrontation? Suddenly, Henya recognized the first stranger, now that his false beard had been removed.

"Sheftel!" she cried out in surprise.

This awoke Reb Zaidel who soon sized up the situation. He looked at his guest with profound disappointment. Sheftel replaced each item on the table. Then he fell to his knees, begging for the forgiveness of his hosts. He promised never again to repeat such an evil sin and showed true remorse with bitter tears.

"If we cannot forgive him, how can we expect the Supreme Judge to forgive our shortcomings and grant us a child?" Reb Zaidel thought aloud, still hoping Eliyahu Hanavi would make his appearance tonight. He bade Sheftel go in peace.

Sheftel left with many apologies and thanks, but the second stranger remained. When the door finally closed behind him, the stranger spoke.

48

"I heard your reasoning, Reb Zaidel, for granting forgiveness to Sheftel. May I pray to our Merciful G-d for realization of this, your greatest desire?"

"Certainly," said Reb Zaidel without much thought to this man's words. He was still overwhelmed by all that had transpired.

The stranger wished the couple a good *Yom Tov* and assured them that Hashem would fulfill their desire. He walked out of the house and closed the door behind him.

Just then Henya jumped up from the couch, a wonderful insight dawning on her.

"How could this man have been so certain? What was he doing here? Who else could he have been but —"

Henya was almost afraid to say the words.

"Perhaps you are right," said Reb Zaidel slowly, beginning to understand the events of the evening. Then as the supposition began to seem more possible, he bolted for the door, opened it and ran to find the man. He returned shortly, face pale and eyes wide.

"Henya," he said in a whisper. "The man has simply disappeared!"

The couple was certain this had indeed been Eliyahu Hanavi when within the very same year Henya gave birth to a son.

The Manuscript

The Manuscript

IT WAS NIGHTTIME IN VILNA, and along the city streets the flickering lanterns threw black ominous shadows everywhere. The townspeople had long since retired for the night. The children were safely tucked into their beds. The horses slept in their stalls. No one but an occasional night watchman stalked the streets at this hour.

Emerging from the shadows of an alleyway trudged Ivan the Peddler from Polnia. His back was bent under the weight of the bundle slung over his shoulder. He was tired, hungry and frustrated.

All day long he had knocked on doors bearing the Jewish *mezuzah* on their posts, offering his merchandise. His partner in Polnia had taught him this trick of identifying potential customers. Yet he had not even made a single sale. The few Jews who did take an interest in his books and examined them only proceeded to insult him, casting doubt on their authenticity. Either the Jews of Vilna had never heard this author, thought Ivan the Peddler, or they did not think very highly of him.

Ivan was bitterly disappointed. When his supplier had given him these manuscripts of Biblical commentary in Polnia he had assured him they would command a kingly sum. Though Vilna was distant, it was a major Jewish center where their value would certainly be appreciated. Ivan had taken the manuscripts on consignment. It was agreed that Ivan would keep seventy-five percent of the profits for his troubles in travelling so far.

Ivan had begun the journey with great enthusiasm, but now that he was finally in Vilna and penniless, he was thoroughly disgusted with the whole idea. He didn't even have any money left to pay for lodging and something to eat. Having nowhere to go, he wandered aimlessly through the streets, grumbling to himself as he dragged his feet along.

The hour grew late, and one by one the lighted windows in each home grew dark. Surely all the town is sleeping by now, while my poor legs carry me nowhere, Ivan thought bitterly, as he stopped to survey the quiet street he had come upon.

Of all the buildings there, only one remained illuminated. This was the local *Bais Medrash,* which was open to any Jew at any time. When Ivan recognized the *mezuzah* on the doorpost he understood this to be a Jewish establishment. In all fairness, he felt the Jews were responsible for his lodging. After all, it was their sacred writings he shouldered mile after mile. Ivan decided to enter these doors and demand a good hot meal and a comfortable bed from the Jews within. He'd threaten to burn the holy manuscripts right then and there if they denied him these basic needs. He had no use for the manuscripts anyway; all they meant to him was an extra twenty pounds on his back.

Thus resolved, Ivan pushed open the doors prepared to lash out his threat to whoever stood on the other side. To his surprise, he only faced hundreds more books lining the walls and stacked upon the tables. There were benches and two platforms. Suspended over one of these platforms was the burning lamp he had seen from the street. A large table covered with a velvet cloth stood upon the other. Ivan eyed the tin box standing on the table.

"Hello," he called out. Only the high ceiling returned his greeting with an echo. Stealthily, Ivan moved forward, peering through the aisles of benches. There was no one there but him.

He reached the platform in the center of the room and he dropped his bundle. He picked up the tin box and heard the rattle of coins within. It was obviously a charity box, and its heaviness indicated it was full.

"This," he said aloud, "is indeed a fair trade. Now I shall harbor no ill feelings towards the Jews of Vilna, for they will unwittingly pay me well for these books. I have even done them the service of delivery directly to their library. We are even."

Well satisfied, Ivan turned to leave. He walked out and gently closed the doors behind him. The box was concealed under his greatcoat, but already Ivan had removed a few coins and jingled them happily in his pocket as he made his way to the nearest inn.

He had only gone one block when he met two bearded figures walking in the opposite direction. They eyed him curiously. Ivan merely lifted his chin and moved on at a hurried pace as the coins in the box clanked even louder. It didn't take long for the two scholars to reach the *Bais Medrash* and discover the *pushka* stolen. They had stepped out for only a few minutes. The *pushka* must have been taken by the suspicious man they had passed just minutes before. They ran out to find him, but he was nowhere in sight. Ivan was already sitting comfortably behind a table at the inn.

Word of the stolen charity box spread quickly. By morning, almost the entire Jewish community was aware of it. Some people speculated that the suspicious man seen walking in the street the previous night must have been the peddler whose manuscripts they had rejected only the day before. The horseless peddler most certainly spent the night at a local inn, they surmised. It was unlikely he'd leave Vilna on foot in the dark. Throughout the city, Jewish men posted themselves at the door of each inn, awaiting his departure.

Ivan awoke late the next morning feeling quite groggy. He remembered feasting on goose with potatoes, cracking many nuts and drinking more than a few glasses of wine. He had sung till he was hoarse and then staggered up to this big comfortable bed. But now there was a dull pain in his head, and his ears rang constantly. Slowly, he got up and dressed. Then he went down to pay his bill. He reached into his pocket for the change jingling there, but when it was counted it did not suffice.

"Wait a moment," Ivan told the clerk. He ran back up the steps to get the tin box and his coat. He returned shortly and paid the balance from the box. He turned to go, swinging his coat over his shoulders, concealing the box in its woolen folds, as he walked out the door.

"Halt!" cried a voice at his side. "Hand over that box!"

Ivan looked up to face a tall Jewish man. Immediately, he was surrounded by four more angry Jews.

"Thief!" cried the first man. "We shall bring you to the baron in the name of justice. Hand over that box now!"

Overwhelmed, Ivan obeyed. In stony silence the party walked into Baron Rupski's palace. Curious onlookers followed, wondering what business these five prestigious Jews could have with a simple peddler. By the time they reached the castle gates a crowd of curious onlookers had formed. The sentry allowed the people to pass after a few moments, but once in the courtyard, they were told to wait until the Baron appeared on the veranda.

Baron Rupski was an old respected general who had fought many victorious battles. The king had granted him vast estates in the city of Vilna in appreciation of his loyal service throughout the years. The general was kindly disposed toward all the citizenry; he was known to be a fair and honest landowner. Yet, he struck fear into the hearts of all who had the misfortune to be brought to justice before him. For he showed no mercy to criminals. If he found the defendant guilty, his wrath knew no bounds. The Jews of Vilna were confident Ivan would be dealt with justly.

Baron Rupski stepped out onto the veranda overlooking the courtyard. He surveyed the party below, a strange gentile peddler surrounded by his loyal Jewish subjects. He nodded his head at the tall Jew who had first discovered Ivan leaving the inn.

"Speak Isaac," he said. "What is your claim?"

Yitzchak stepped forward, bowed respectfully, and cleared his throat.

"Yesterday," he said, "this peddler approached many of my colleagues as well as myself with some manuscripts. He was unable to convince us of their value and was consequently unable to make a sale. Later in the evening, he entered our House of Study and removed the charity box. Clearly, he is a dishonest peddler who has turned to thievery."

The baron studied the defendant.

"What is your name?" he asked. "And from where do you come?"

Ivan proudly raised his eyes to the baron.

"My name is Ivan Kurok," he replied. "I come from Polnia."

"What is your business in Vilna, then?"

"My supplier had commissioned me to sell Hebrew manuscripts to the Jews here, for a fair profit."

"What type of manuscripts?" The baron asked.

"I. . . I don't understand their content. . ." stammered Ivan.

"Then how could you expect to earn a profit as a reputable salesman?" demanded Baron Rupski.

Ivan was defeated. He made no reply.

The baron sighed hopelessly.

"Well," he said, "is it true that you stole the charity box from the House of Study?"

Ivan answered quickly.

"I'm not a thief," he insisted. "I haven't stolen anything."

"Is there evidence?" asked the baron turning to Yitzchak.

"Yes," came the reply as Yitzchak produced the tin charity box. "This was found on the peddler and handed over to me in the presence of many witnesses."

"Is this true?"

"Yes, it is true," admitted Ivan. "But the box was not stolen. I left the valuable manuscripts in its place. As a fair trade."

"Where exactly did you leave them?"

"Upon the covered table in the House of Study."

The baron clapped his hands, and a servant instantly appeared. He was dispatched with instructions to fetch the manuscripts and bring them to the baron.

The baron faced his audience and continued.

"I have visited Polnia many times throughout my career as a general. I am familiar with the name of any important person who has resided there in the past fifty years. I will hand the manuscripts to you, Isaac, and you will read aloud the author's name. If I do indeed recognize it as that of a celebrated personality, at least we will have established the authenticity of the books. And Ivan's honesty as a peddler. But if," the baron's voice grew low and threatening, "the name is unfamiliar to me I shall punish Ivan severely. Yes, severely indeed."

Ivan closed his eyes and prayed in his heart that his supplier had not betrayed him with a worthless manuscript. Soon the courier returned panting, carrying the heavy load. The baron signaled from the veranda that he hand it directly to Yitzchak.

Yitzchak opened the top volume and read aloud, "*Toldos Yaakov Yosef.* This has been written by a Rabbi Yaakov Yosef."

"Rabbi Yaakov Yosef?" the baron cried suddenly jumping to his feet.

"Rabbi Yaakov Yosef," Yitzchak confirmed as he opened the next book.

The baron's face paled, and he excused himself for a few minutes. A servant helped him inside, and he collapsed onto the couch. He dismissed the servant, leaving instructions that he wished to be left alone for a while.

This was indeed the turning point in his life he had anticipated. He now stood on the threshold of death. No, he could not withhold the fair judgment his subjects sought, for then he would deny the principles of justice for which he had fought valiantly all his life. Yet, by settling this issue he would be pronouncing his own death sentence. Well, he could not hold back the hands of time; these events were destined to be. He would not fight the Will of the Jewish G-d. Yes, he had lived a glorious life and would be buried in satisfied old age. He hoped G-d would reward him with an equally wonderful afterlife.

With renewed strength, Baron Rupski lifted himself up and summoned his servant. He returned to the veranda, and an instant hush fell upon the people. The baron requested their patience and full attention throughout the seemingly unrelated narrative he was about to begin.

"Many years ago," he began, "my regiment camped outside the city of Polnia for one night. When morning came and the bugle was sounded, I discovered three of my soldiers missing.

"Immediately, I organized a search party to comb the city. Shortly, they returned with a strange story. The party hadn't gone very far, and already they had discovered the soldiers.

"'So why haven't you brought them back with you?' I demanded impatiently. 'Don't you realize it is late and we must move on?'

"'It is impossible,' came the breathless reply. 'They are standing in the dining room of a small home not far from here. There is an old man with a long white beard sitting at the head of the table in meditation. Our soldiers stand as if glued to the floor beneath them, moving not a muscle.'

"I found it hard to believe this so I sent a second contingent of my most trusted men. They too, returned with the same amazing report. By now I was mystified enough to visit this home myself. I chose two of the soldiers of the second party as my escorts and went to investigate. Peering through the window, I found everything exactly as described by my soldiers. Only they couldn't possibly relate the wonder inspired by the presence of this holy man of G-d. His face was alight with mystical radiance. His eyes glowed with intense fervor. Obviously, this man could see dimensions of other spiritual spheres invisible to lesser men like myself. I watched him, transfixed, until I reminded myself of the purpose of my visit. I summoned all my courage to approach this saint and disturb his concentration. I remember well how ironic I thought this was. Here I stood, a fearless general who had faced the enemy countless times in mortal combat, and now a harmless old Jew inspired in me an awesome fear I had never felt before.

"As politely as I could, I interrupted the rabbi's thoughts. I explained that the soldiers standing motionless in the room belonged to my regiment. Perhaps he could release them so we could continue on our way in peace.

"'As soon as their pockets are emptied of the precious items they have removed from the table, they will be free to move about?' said the rabbi.

"With the assistance of my escorts, the valuables were found and returned to the table. This accomplished, two of the soldiers blinked their eyes and flexed their stiffened muscles. They looked about them, and embarrassed, shuffled their way outside to wait. The third soldier still stood frozen in his place. Helplessly, I turned to the rabbi.

"The Rabbi shrugged. 'Perhaps he still has a trinket hidden on his person,' he suggested.

"I searched the soldier personally and found a small silver goblet hidden under his shirt. As soon as it was removed, the soldier's vitality was restored. He too, went outside to join the rest of the guilty party. I bade my escorts follow. Now I remained alone in the room with the rabbi.

"'I would like to apologize,' I told him, 'for the misbehavior of my soldiers. I was certainly unaware of their evil scheme and am most grateful to you for apprehending them, as they well deserved.'

"The Rabbi waved his hand and shook his head. 'You are mistaken,' he said. 'It was not I who held them back, but G-d.'

"'But in what merit, then, have you earned His divine protection?' I asked.

"The rabbi smiled and then explained, 'The merit of the forefathers of our people. You see, many years ago G-d found them worthy of redemption from Egyptian slavery. It is on this very night of Passover, our *Lail Shimurim*, the Night of G-d's Watch, that we keep our doors unlocked to show our complete faith in His protection.'

"'I am beginning to understand,' I said slowly. 'Tonight you celebrated the holiday with a feast and adorned the table with your precious silver utensils —'

"'To make us feel like kings in both physical as well as spiritual wealth,' the rabbi finished my sentence. 'My family had long since gone to sleep, and I remained here to read some more about the wonders of the Passover miracles. I was so engrossed I hardly heard the soldiers at the door. I must have made their scheme so easy until —'

"'Do not bother, Rabbi,' I said. 'I can imagine what happened next. Your G-d immediately executed justice upon the soldiers just as they completed their crime.'

"We both smiled.

"'You see, I take personal pleasure in all this because I am a lover of justice.' I said.

"'Then rejoice,' said the rabbi, 'in the knowledge that all the world bows to the Supreme Justice of G-d. Though as mortal men we often cannot fathom the justice in seemingly twisted fate, believe me it is always there. We only see part of the puzzle, but G-d is the Master of all the pieces. G-d is perfect, and the world He created is perfect.'

"I remained silent a short while as I thought this over. Finally I looked up at the Rabbi's kind face and said, "You are by far the holiest man I have ever met. Please bless me.'

"'What do you desire?' Asked the Rabbi.

"'I am childless,' I said softly. 'I wish for a son.'

"'You will be blessed with sons,' the Rabbi said simply. 'What else do you wish?'

"I hesitated to admit my fear, but in this moment of truth I bared my heart to the rabbi.

"'Bless me with long life," I said. 'As a general, any day of war may be my last, and I fear the grave.'

The rabbi showed no sign of surprise. He merely shook his head, 'You will live to a ripe old age,' he assured me.

"'Then tell me one more thing,' I begged. 'What age will that be?'

"'This cannot be told to any mortal at any time,' the Rabbi said, his voice rising. 'But this much I will tell you. One day it will come to pass that you will be called upon to reveal my worth to Jews of a distant city. When you have accomplished this task you will know that your days on this earth will soon come to an end.'

"'What is your name, then?' I asked.

"'Yaakov Yosef of Polnia,' the Rabbi said simply. 'This is all you need to know.'

"He walked me to the door. I grasped his hand in appreciation, and we bade each other farewell."

Baron Rupski paused, and looked heavenward. Then he declared as loudly as his proud voice carried, "I have been blessed by the Jewish G-d with four good sons. I have been

blessed by the Jewish G-d with a long happy life."

The baron then fell silent for a long moment. Finally he continued, "It would comfort me much to know that I have done credit to the name of Yaakov Yosef. I urge you now to study his works, and through them you will surely come to appreciate the greatness of their author. Pay Ivan, as he deserves the amount he already spent from the charity box. Use the books well."

The baron bowed graciously and backed off the veranda. He collapsed into the arms of the servant that stood there.

"I'm exhausted," he murmured. "So exhausted."

Ivan let out a sigh of relief and uttered a prayer of thankfulness to the Jewish G-d for the sacred manuscripts.

Moishke the Tailor

Moishke the Tailor

T HE WINTER HAD BEEN LONG AND COLD. *Pesach* was approaching, and still, there were tremendous snow-drifts and icy roadways. Moishke's little children huddled around the oven while his wife Baila stirred the breakfast porridge. The door opened with a blast of cold air, and Moishke appeared. Everyone shivered, and quickly the heavy door was pushed shut.

Moishke was a tailor. He would take his satchel of equipment and go from town to town looking for work, any work, from mending small items to sewing entire suits of clothing. He was gone from the house all week long, only returning home *Erev Shabbos*. He'd dispense his earnings then, ten percent for *tzedakah* and the rest for his wife Baila to run the household. If there ever was anything left over after the bills were paid she would set it aside for the extra expenses of the following *Yom Tov*.

This *Yom Tov* of *Pesach*, however, had no cushioned credit beneath it. Times were difficult for everyone in the bitter winter. Moishke had to work doubly hard to make ends meet. He'd venture out in the extreme cold on foot and walk for miles until he found work, knocking on doors in distant villages. What *menuchah* he found when he came home to rest for *Shabbos* in his own bed! All the week's work was forgotten in the warm glow of the *Shabbos* candles. Moishke would spend most of the day in the *Bais Medrash* where he'd indulge himself in the study of *Torah*. Thus spiritually fortified, he felt encouraged to go out again on Sunday for another week of hard work.

Now another Sunday had arrived along with another snowstorm. Moishke was returning from the little *Bais Hamedrash* where he davened *Shacharis* on Sunday mornings. It promised to be a difficult week.

"Good morning!" Moishke said briskly to his family, stamping his feet and rubbing his hands. "It's cold out there! You'd never think *Pesach* was coming with weather like this!"

He sat down on the wooden bench next to the tiny table and told his family of the great snow outside.

"It's so deep," said Moishke, bending down and drawing his face close to little Raizel's eyes, "that you'd be stuck in snow up to your chin!"

Everyone laughed.

"But Moishke," asked Baila as she placed the steaming bowls on the table, "how can you possibly travel in weather like this?"

Moishke sighed.

"Anything's possible when it's necessary," he said.

Time spent at home with the family always passed much too quickly, and almost before he knew it, Moishke had to pack up and leave. He put on the patched overcoat and took up the satchel filled with his tools and threads. He kissed each one of his children goodbye, telling them to be good and to listen to their mother. Baila wished him *mazel* and *hatzlachah*, luck and success, with special emphasis. Moishke understood her message. She hoped he would make out especially well this week to meet the expenses for the *matzoh* and wine she had ordered.

Shaking his head, Moishke climbed down the rickety steps of the front porch. He drew his coat more closely around his neck as the sharp winds attacked. The snow was deep, literally up to his knees, and already hardened from the drop in temperature. Each step was accomplished with great difficulty, raising his legs high and plunging them down into the frozen drifts. But there was nothing to be done except move slowly along toward the main road where hopefully conditions would be better.

Moishke hopped on, carrying his *Tallis* and *Teffilin* in a bundle held to his chest while his satchel bounced up and down as it lay strapped across his back. At least I've got one arm free for balance, he thought. Suddenly his foot caught and he tripped. Moishke fell into the snow with both hands outstretched in front of him. Bent over in this position, groping for his fallen *Tefillin*, he heard the snorting sounds of horses and the jingling of bells.

Moishke glanced up, and with dread he recognized the gilded carriage of his merciless landlord, Count Pavel Czernowiecki. The carriage came to a sudden stop, and the cruel man seated inside stuck out his head. Moishke could see the kind face of the countess in the interior of the carriage.

"Oh, it is only you, Moishke," the landlord called with a sneer. "I bade the driver stop, certain I'd found a fox to shoot. Well, you do look like one, crawling in the snow that way."

The landlord turned to his wife.

"He does look like a fox, wouldn't you say my dear?" he asked loudly.

Without waiting for a reply he turned back to Moishke.

"Yes, I am disappointed, but fear not," he said. "All is not lost. For you see, you make excellent target practice. Hold still a minute as I aim my gun —"

By this time Moishke had found his *Tefillin* and gotten to his feet. He came close to the carriage.

"Don't! Please don't shoot!" he begged. "I have a wife and children."

"Get down right now on all fours or I'll go after them, too!" snarled Sir Pavel. His breath reeked with alcohol.

Moishke trembled and bent down, crying out the *Sh'ma* and clutching his *Tefillin*. A volley of bullets flew by high above his head and far off to the side. Sir Pavel took a moment to reload his rifle and grumble his curses while Moishke uttered all of the *Viduy* he could remember. He prayed that Hashem have mercy on the widowed wife and orphaned children he'd leave behind just as another shrill shot hissed by.

"That's enough!" cried the countess, grabbing the arm that held the rifle. "That's enough!"

"Aw, leave me alone! You know I won't kill him. I'm just having some sport."

"You'll frighten him to death in just another moment!" cried Lady Clara. "Already he's motionless, frozen with fear."

"Okay, I'll leave him, for your sake," said Pavel grudgingly, putting the rifle away. "He's a lucky Jew to have such an ally."

"You're drunk," said Lady Clara. "Get back into the carriage."

Lady Clara signalled, and the wagon driver got down from his seat. He opened the door and helped Sir Pavel climb in.

"What'll we do with the Jew?" Lady Clara asked the driver. "I'm certain he's in a state of shock, and my husband is responsible for him. What should we do?"

"Leave him there," mumbled the landlord from inside the carriage. "Those Jews are blessed with strong physical constitutions. Their G-d always helps."

Lady Clara ignored this and had the driver lift the unconscious Moishke into the carriage.

"At least put him outside, with the driver," protested Pavel sluggishly. He was growing increasingly senseless from the alcohol in his blood.

This, too, Lady Clara ignored, and Moishke was laid on the floor inside, with a cushion under his head. Sir Pavel growled and grumbled himself to sleep as the carriage rhythmically pulled on, its heavy sleighs crunching against the hard snow.

Soon Moishke stirred and awoke. He was confused. There lay his landlord snoring loudly, and here sat his wife looking through the window of their carriage. What was he, Moishke the Tailor, doing here? Then Lady Clara turned her head and smiled kindly, and suddenly the memory of the shooting spree came back to him. Moishke's first thought was to thank Hashem for mercifully sparing his life.

Lady Clara politely asked Moishke how he felt and apologized for her husband's careless behavior. She explained that they were returning to the castle where the family doctor would check his health.

Moishke assured her he felt fine. It would be more helpful if the driver stopped to let him out now before Sir Pavel awoke. He felt strong enough to continue on his way.

"But where were you going on foot in such deep snow?" inquired Lady Clara.

"About my business," Moishke answered simply.

"What is this trade that requires you to travel even on days such as this?" asked Lady Clara with wide eyes.

Moishke explained that he was a tailor, how he made his small income and how his wife ran the house. He spoke of the approaching holiday and the need to earn additional money to cover expenses. This was why he was so anxious to hop down from the carriage this very minute and go back on his way.

"Wait a moment," Lady Clara said thoughtfully. "Perhaps I can employ you. Stay here in the carriage till we reach the castle. I insist the doctor examine you. If he confirms your good health I will commission you to do some mending for me. Today."

So it was. Moishke was declared healthy, and Lady Clara gave him enough work to keep him busy till evening. When he finished she inspected the garments he repaired, examining the close neat stitches he set.

"I'm impressed," she said. "You put careful detail into your work."

Lady Clara pressed a purse of five gold coins into his hand.

"Come back next week and I'll have more work for you," she promised.

Moishke thanked her profusely. Imagine! Five gulden. this was what he earned at the end of a good month travelling from town to town. Now he had earned it all in one day! What fortune Hashem had thrown upon him!

Moishke returned home all smiles. His wife was happily surprised to see him, but feared the snow had discouraged him after all. When he told his family all that happened that day, they cheered and clapped delightedly.

"Let us not forget," Moishke called out amidst the joyful noise, "to thank Hashem for the goodness He has sent our way. We must make ourselves worthy of every kindness He gives and will continue to grant."

The week flew by quickly, Moishke spending most of his time in the *Bais Medrash*. His wife already had enough money to pay for the wine and the *matzos*. Perhaps, he thought to himself the next Sunday morning, today I'll earn enough to give Baila money to purchase meat for *Yom Tov*.

Moishke was right. Lady Clara gave him fabric and asked him to sew two sets of clothing for her children. This was plenty of work and Moishke would be paid well, double the

previous week's salary, at the completion of the task. The job
job couldn't possibly be finished by the end of the day, and
so Moishke returned on Monday.

By evening the last pair of trousers were still incomplete.
Moishke promised to take it home and finish it there. He
explained to Lady Clara that in just two more days the
Pesach holiday would commence and his wife needed his
help at home. Lady Clara admired Moishke's consideration
for his wife and graciously let him go.

It was early the next morning when Moishke returned to
the castle. He had worked till late in the night to finish the
trousers, and now he was proud of his accomplishment. He
was confident Lady Clara would be pleased.

However, it was not she who greeted him in the breakfast room after the maid bade him enter; it was her husband
Sir Pavel who sat there smirking at him.

"So it's you, Moishke!" he roared with a great bellowing
laugh. "I see you're alive after all!"

"Yes," answered Moishke quietly. "My G-d had mercy on
me and spared my life."

"I see," said Sir Pavel. "So I see. He has spared the breath
of your life. But does your G-d care to keep it going? Has he
provided you with a decent livelihood?"

Sir Pavel pointed to Moishke's worn boots and patched
coat. He rolled with laughter.

"Yes," Moishke said proudly, standing his ground. "My
G-d gives all life and sustains all life."

Sir Pavel ceased to laugh and sat upright in his chair. He
leveled his eyes at Moishke. He frowned, displeased.

"My G-d does this, and my G-d does that," he mocked.
"That is what you say all the time, and I'm getting quite tired
of it. Well, according to my wife, it is she who has been
providing your income."

"But it is G-d who sees fit to give her what to pay!" said
Moishke zealously.

"Again we come back to your G-d!" roared the landlord.
"How do you expect to raise the money for your holiday if

my generous wife doesn't pay you?" shouted Sir Pavel triumphantly.

"My G-d will not abandon those worthy of his sustenance," replied Moishke instinctively. "He can put it into anyone's heart to pay for my work, and anyone will provide my salary."

This remark so insulted the landlord that he took the rifle from the wall and pointed its barrel between Moishke's eyes.

"Out with you!" he stormed. "Don't ever step onto this property again or I'll make my dinner from your flesh."

Moishke dropped the package with the trousers on the floor and fled. He was halfway out the gate when Sir Pavel bellowed, "Let your G-d pay you the ten gulden my wife promised!"

Moishke came home short of breath. A pallor of black disappointment colored his features. His wife listened quietly as Moishke related the conversation with Sir Pavel.

"Perhaps I spoke too quickly without thought," said Moishke regretfully. "Now I have thrown away the opportunity Hashem has granted us to make a decent *Pesach*."

"Not so," countered Baila. "Two good things have come out of this. First, you have made a *Kiddush Hashem*, demonstrating your undiluted faith in the One G-d Who provides for all. Second, we have learned firsthand not to depend on people for our sustenance, whether kindly inclined or not. Perhaps it is better this way, for it strengthens our awareness that we are dependent on Hashem."

Moishke nodded his head. Yes, his good wife was right. He rolled up his sleeves and asked her how he might help out for *Yom Tov*. That evening would already be *Bedikas Chametz*. Baila put her husband to work, and the financial loss was forgotten in the busy bustle of the *Pesach* preparations.

Evening came, and Moishke took his candle and feather and went about the house. The children followed behind. Suddenly, the door flew open, and a foul smelling bundle was thrown in. Moishke put down the candle as his face paled. He recognized the powerful stench of a corpse. What else could this mean *Erev Pesach* but the workings of a blood libel?

"Baila!" he called in panic. "I must run this very minute to the *Rav*. There's no time to spare."

"Wait a moment!" said Baila. "Maybe we ought to open the bundle before you go."

"There is no time," mumbled Moishke as he put on his coat. "You always think we have all the time in the world."

Baila opened the bundle herself.

"Look Moishke!" she exclaimed. "It's only a monkey!"

Moishke drew the candle near and looked over her shoulder in wonder. Indeed, it was only a dead monkey. Who sent this and why? thought Moishke. But now was not the time to ponder. Better throw this unclean animal outside immediately. He quickly gathered up the cloth in which it was wrapped, and a gold coin jingled to the floor.

Now Moishke was really amazed. He asked Baila to hand him the *traifah* knife as his excitement mounted. Moishke neatly severed the animal's chest. Sure enough, there lay a treasure of gold coins!

In the morning, Moishke went to buy meat, fish and other foodstuffs for *Pesach*. He brought home presents of clothing for Baila and the children and beautiful things with which to adorn the *Seder*.

Two guests joined Moishke and his family for *Pesach*. Everyone had a place at the table, set with his own silver cup and *Haggadah*. Moishke sat at the head, leaning back on his splendid new pillow. That night he experienced the real joy of freedom, such as he had never been able to feel in years past. He could truly imagine himself as a royal prince of Hashem, and so he led the *Seder* in supreme holiness.

They reached *Shefoch Chamaschah*, and little Raizel ran to open the door. And who should be standing there gazing inside? It was none other than Sir Pavel himself with Lady Clara at his side.

Awkwardly, Moishke invited them in. They both took a seat and listened quietly as Moishke finished the *Seder*. He felt most uncomfortable, and though he could hardly admit it to himself, his knees trembled under the long white *kittel*. When the last praises were finally sung and Baila began to clear the table, Sir Pavel cleared his throat to speak.

"I took Lady Clara for a walk, intending to find your house dark, bare of festivity," he said. "How is it possible that you have set so lavish a table with so many bright candles?"

"My G-d has not forsaken me. He has provided all you see."

Moishke then told the miraculous story of the strange monkey.

Sir Pavel could not contain himself.

"Yes, yes, I know about the dead monkey. I had it sent to you as a present for your holiday. But I knew nothing of the gold coins inside it. Something has been happening in my own palace without my knowledge." His face blackened and his temper rose. "I must investigate the matter immediately. Come, Lady Clara. We must seek out the traitor among our staff and warrant his due punishment."

Lady Clara perceived the dangerous note in her husband's voice. Perhaps he would go home and shoot one of the servants!

"One moment," she said. "Calm down. There's no reason to upset yourself so. I can explain everything."

All eyes turned to Lady Clara who smiled to herself, savoring the secret.

"Speak already!" demanded Sir Pavel.

"Well," she said, folding her hands on her lap. "Don't you recall, my good husband, a sack filled with coins you received in payment of a loan? I had the treasurer determine if they were indeed genuine gold by taking one out and biting into it. You know how our monkey always loved to imitate. Well, she too wanted to taste those beautiful golden delicacies. So she did, swallowing one after the other until she made herself sick, and —"

Sir Pavel broke into great peels of laughter. What an amusing little character the monkey had been, even up to her very death. Sir Pavel laughed and laughed till the tears poured from his eyes. When he was finally able to control himself, he turned to Moishke.

"I'm forced to admit you were right all along," he said. "Your G-d has not abandoned you. When He sees fit for us to give, willingly or not, we give. Let us now leave you in peace."

Sir Pavel rose. He looked around at the room drenched in golden candlelight, at the silver cups and bottles gleaming on the white linen tablecloth. He looked at Moishke the Tailor, dressed in white, enthroned on his satin pillows, surrounded by his family and his guests. At that moment, Moishke's face shone with a majesty greater than Sir Pavel had ever seen in the palaces of Warsaw.

"Come, Lady Clara," said Sir Pavel in a suddenly humble voice. "Let us return to the castle and let these good people continue their festivities."

Before she walked out the door Lady Clara turned around.

"I'm sure Sir Pavel won't mind if you come back to work for me after your holiday," she said to Moishke.

"How can I deny you, Lady Clara," said Sir Pavel, shaking his head, "especially when it's the Will of Moishke's G-d, too?"

The Perfect Host

The Perfect Host

T HE WORLD WAS WHITE WITH SNOW, but the serene beauty belied the havoc underneath. The snow covered every road, every path, every byway, immobilizing all traffic. The air grew colder day by day, lending perman- ence to snowbanks and ice sheets. It would be many weeks before the sun warmed the heavens and thawed the earth.

Among the hundreds of travellers stranded far from home was the Jewish merchant Ovadiah Shatz. He had left his wife and children not long after *Sukkos*, as he did every year, and travelled to the winter trade fair in distant Zhabnitz. Ovadiah usually spent the winter months in Zhabnitz, where he earned enough to sustain his family for the entire year. Ovadiah was almost always home by *Purim*, or at worst a week after, but this year *Purim* had found him still trapped by the snows in Zhabnitz.

He had set out for home shortly after *Purim*. Although severe snowstorms had made his progress painfully slow, Ovadiah clung to the hope of spending the *Sedarim* with his family.

Day followed day, week followed week, and still Ovadiah found himself amidst unfamiliar snow-covered towns and villages. *Pesach* drew ever closer, and Ovadiah despaired of returning home in time. It would take at least three days journey to get home under the best conditions, he calculated as he watched the howling winds and dropping temperatures from the window of a common inn. Even if the roads opened tomorrow existing conditions would stretch the trip to a week, and there were just three days left until *Bedikas Chametz*. It seemed he would have to spend *Pesach* in this strange town. Ovadiah doubted there were any Jewish people living there; he had seen none during the few days he had been stranded there.

With a sigh, Ovadiah left the window for the innkeeper's office down the corridor. He would have to make arrangements to reserve his room for at least another week.

This task accomplished, Ovadiah set out on foot to seek provisions for *Pesach*. Eggs and potatoes would certainly be available on one of the neighboring farms, he thought. He put on his boots and braced himself to face the bitter cold. He wrapped his coat about him as the winds tore at him. He was the only person walking through the snow, in defiance of the elements. Loneliness and depression engulfed him.

Ovadiah looked up at the horizon and saw the smoke of a chimney curling up to the sky. Perhaps it was a farm. Ovadiah plunged forward in the direction of the chimney smoke, anxious to make the necessary purchases. Perhaps the farmer even had horseradish, he dared to hope.

It was indeed a farm. Ovadiah pushed the white gate over the pile of snow till the opening was wide enough for him to push through. Once in the farmyard, he looked about at the sprawling farmhouse, large barn and a separate chicken coop. The farmer was obviously well to do. Still somehow, the general overview did not impress Ovadiah as a reflection of wealthy affluence.

Ovadiah climbed up the porch and tugged at a rope attached to a wrought iron bell. Shortly, the door was opened by a smiling woman in an apron with a kerchief covering her hair. Could it be possible? Quickly Ovadiah glanced at the doorpost, and yes! A *mezuzah!* What good fortune Hashem had sent him!

"*Shalom Aleichem!*" Ovadiah nearly shouted, bursting with joy.

"Come in, come in!" came the warm reply.

Ovadiah thumped his boots against the doorpost, leaving as much snow as possible outside.

"Don't worry!" said the woman. "I'm cleaning for *Pesach* anyway. Snow is not even *chametz!*"

Ovadiah laughed heartily. It had been so long since he had heard Yiddish spoken. Alone in unfamiliar surroundings he had not expected to hear anyone speak of *Pesach* or *chametz*. Yet here was a Jewish household undergoing preparation for *Yom Tov!* Perhaps he would not have to spend *Pesach* by himself after all. Of course, it would never be the same as sitting at his own *Seder* table with his wife Esther and the children, but it would be *Pesach* nevertheless, with wine, *matzos* and a friendly family.

"Shmuel!" called the woman. "Come quick. We have an important guest."

Ovadiah heard the clatter of pots from the cellar and soon the quick leap of footsteps up the stairs.

"*Bruchim Habaim!*" the host exclaimed, enthusiastically shaking Ovadiah's hand. "From where are you coming?"

Ovadiah then explained his business, how the snowstorm had interfered with his plans for *Yom Tov* and then he went on to explain the purpose of his visit to the farm.

"I only hoped to purchase some eggs and potatoes to take back to my room," he concluded with a smile."I hardly dared hope you might even have some horseradish —"

"Don't be silly," interrupted the host."You'll join us for all eight days of *Yom Tov*. I'll personally see to your every comfort."

"Thank you, thank you," gushed Ovadiah."It was bad enough being separated from my family for *Pesach*. I couldn't bear the thought of spending *Yom Tov* by myself in an inn amongst *goyim*."

"There is one thing I have to ask you," said the farmer, giving Ovadiah a speculative look.

"Certainly, certainly," said Ovadiah."I will do anything to help for *Yom Tov*."

"I want you to pay me two hundred rubles."

Ovadiah was taken aback. Two hundred rubles! That was half of what he had earned over the entire winter. He had intended to give his wife thirty rubles for all of *Pesach*, a sum sufficient to cover every expense from wine to clothing, even *afikomen* gifts. And here he stood, a victim of circumstances, seeking hospitality on strange territory. His hosts had seemed warm, decent people. Why were they trying to take advantage of his desperate situation?

"Perhaps," Ovadiah suggested uncomfortably, "you would accept fifty rubles as a reasonable payment?"

The host moved forward, drew himself to his full height and squared his shoulders. He looked sharply into Ovadiah's eyes and the corners of his mouth turned down.

"Two hundred rubles, not a kopek less!" he said in a low, deliberate tone. "You may take three dozen eggs and a large sack of potatoes and return to your inn if you wish. I will let you decide."

There wasn't much of a decision to make, for the lonely inn was hardly an alternative.

"I will pay your price," said Ovadiah hastily, wishing to restore the friendly atmosphere.

"Good, good!" Shmuel beamed, his manner relaxing. All this while, his wife had stood meekly in the corner. Now she stepped forward and welcomed Ovadiah graciously. She clapped her hands, and a serving girl appeared. She was given instructions to prepare Ovadiah's room.

A second servant was summoned. He was told to go to the inn, pay up Ovadiah's bill and return with his possessions. Ovadiah protested. These were his personal responsibilities, but his host insisted.

"You are my guest now," he said with a smile, "and this service is my pleasure."

Ovadiah was led to the kitchen where he was given a good hot meal. He complimented his hostess on her hearty cooking and thanked her for making him feel so at home. Shmuel sat down on the other side of the table and started asking him all about his business and the town from which he hailed. Ovadiah took the opportunity to inquire about *Yiddishkeit* in this country region. He learned to his great surprise that there was a *minyan* not too far away, made up of farmers such as Shmuel.

The servant returned and showed Ovadiah to his room. Fresh linens and towels were waiting on an enormous bed with an attached stand. A warm fire was burning, and a pitcher of hot tea was set up on the mantlepiece. Ovadiah was overwhelmed by all this thoughtful detail. He began to unpack as he found the closets and drawers empty.

Soon there was a knock at the door and Ovadiah went to open it. Shmuel smiled kindly and asked if there was anything he could do to make his guest comfortable. Perhaps he should lie down for a while. They would be up late tonight making *Bedikas Chametz* over all their property.

So it went. Ovadiah rested well and accompanied Shmuel on his *Bedikah.* He only wondered how things were in his own home. His wife undoubtedly knew why he hadn't come home for *Yom Tov.* It had probably snowed there, too. She would have borrowed enough money from a wealthy neighbor, to make *Pesach,* and with Hashem's help, his family would manage, he consoled himself.

In the morning, the two men trudged through the snow to the *minyan*. By the time they returned, it was quite late, and they immediately burned the *chametz*. In the kitchen the *charossess* was chopped and the *marror* ground. In the cellar the barrels were full of wine and the *Pesach* oven was turning out freshly baked *matzos*.

By midafternoon, the household had settled into the *Yom Tov* atmosphere, and Ovadiah went to his room for a nap. When Ovadiah awoke he found a beautiful suit of clothes hanging in the closet which he hadn't noticed yesterday. A note was pinned to the tunic which read, "*Pesach* garments." There was a silk shirt and a beautiful woolen coat and trousers. There was even an elaborate *kittel* with white on white hand embroidery worked throughout the fabric.

As Ovadiah donned these wonderful clothes, he thought about how much he was paying for this hospitality. He would rather have paid a smaller sum and been satisfied with less. Who needed such luxury at every turn? After all, he was only a simple man.

But when Ovadiah sat at the *Seder* table leaning upon the white satin pillow with the golden *kiddush* cup in his hand he truly felt like a king upon a throne. He was at ease; he was happy; he had much for which to thank Hashem. And so he followed the *Haggadah* with his generous host in supreme glory. In no way did Ovadiah feel inhibited. On the contrary, he had not a care, a responsibility, a worry on his mind. Ovadiah truly felt the *cherus*, the freedom required to serve *Hashem* wholeheartedly. In this wholesome spirit, he celebrated the entire *Yom Tov* with unparalleled enthusiasm.

His hostess served up delicacies he had never tasted, and drinks squeezed from exotic fruits he had never heard of. At every meal there were different varieties of fish, fowl and meat prepared in an elegant sumptuous fashion. And always fruit, nuts and a specialty called chocolate were prepared on the kitchen table.

Though Ovadiah was treated with every luxury, Shmuel and his wife behaved as simple folk. It was true that the house was roomy and filled with furniture, yet it was not gaudy but tastefully fine. Ovadiah wondered why then he had been asked to pay such a great price for such lavish treatment, since it was obviously inconsistent with the personal tastes of his hosts.

At last *Yom Tov* came to an end, and with it came the warming sun. Magically, the snow disappeared, and after *Havdalah* Ovadiah packed to go. He had agreed to pay two hundred rubles for the eight days of *Yom Tov* and did not wish to overstay even one night.

"But it is dangerous to travel in the dark," protested Shmuel. "Please do me a favor and wait till morning. I will let you help us pack away the *Pesach* utensils tonight."

Ovadiah agreed but arose very early the next morning. He was anxious to get back to his family. He found the household quiet. It seemed no one else had yet awakened. He dressed, *davened* and went down to the kitchen. He was surprised to find packages on the table labelled with his name.

He poured himself a cup of coffee and prepared to leave. He sat down and wrote a note to his hosts. He sealed it in an envelope he attached to the purse of two hundred rubles.

"Good morning!" came the voice of Shmuel from behind. "You forgot to take these packages in your haste to leave us. Have we treated you so poorly that you wish to escape without so much as saying goodbye?"

"On the contrary," Ovadiah apologized. "I'm only anxious to return to my family —"

"Without any presents? What of your good wife who made *Pesach* alone? And the children who have waited to ask you the *Mah Nishtanah*? Would you arrive with no gifts for them? I have prepared these for your family in appreciation for the pleasure of your company."

"But you have already lavished me with comforts well

beyond the value of the two hundred rubles you ask. I cannot accept additional gifts," Ovadiah argued, as he handed Shmuel the purse with the envelope.

"What is this?" asked Shmuel raising his hands. "You insult me terribly. Do you want to belittle my *mitzvah* of *Hachnasas Orchim* with petty cash?"

"I don't understand!" murmured Ovadiah, confused. "You only invited me to stay on the condition of two hundred rubles —"

"That was only a ploy of mine," said Shmuel, waving his hand and shaking his head. "I understood that if I were to demand anything less, you would have felt undeserving of our hospitality. You would deprive yourself of the use of fresh linen. You would not let yourself indulge in the *Yom Tov Seudos*. You would have been uncomfortable. You would have felt a great sense of responsibility toward me and so would be unable to speak to me as an equal. This way, we have both fared well. We have shared a beautiful *Yom Tov*. I have earned the *mitzvah* of *Hachnasas Orchim*, and you the willingness to pay for the honor of *Yom Tov* at any price."

It took many moments for Ovadiah to understand and appreciate his host. Finally, he nodded his head.

"You were the perfect host," he said shaking Shmuel's hand and chuckling aloud.

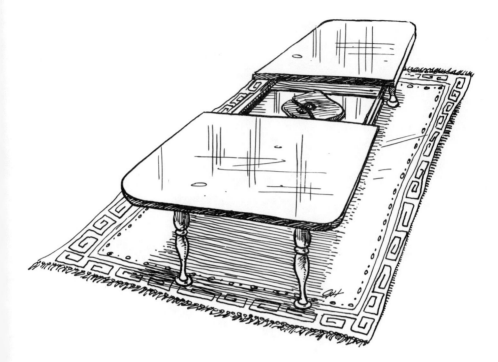

The Missing Pouch

The Missing Pouch

*P*ESACH WAS APPROACHING, and the Rebbetzin hired Sonya, a farmer's wife from the next village, to help with the cleaning. She worked dutifully alongside her mistress, cleaning closets and drawers and scraping out crevices.

Before long, Sonya had gained the confidence of the Rebbetzin and was given specific tasks to do independently. While the Rebbetzin worked in the kitchen, Sonya was put to work in the dining room. She began by dusting the drapes and wiping out the corners of each window sill. After that,

Sonya polished the chairs, getting at the crumbs caught in the scrollwork and upholstery.

Only the table remained to be done. Sonya understood it had to be pulled apart to reach the tiny crumbs between the leaves. At first she thought of calling her mistress to help, but when she peeked into the kitchen and saw the Rebbetzin stooped deep into a cupboard, she thought better of it. She took hold of one end of the table and pulled with all her strength. It moved slightly, and a tiny slit appeared between the two leaves. Sonya went to the other side and grasped the table tightly, but when she jerked it back it strangely slid away from the rest of the table.

Sonya was aghast! Had she broken the table? But no! This was only a slat made to cover a concealed shelf carved into the table. How clever! Sonya reached her hand into the opening and withdrew a heavy leather pouch. It was filled with precious red stones. Just then she heard her mistress closing the cupboard in the kitchen. Sonya thrust the pouch into her apron and replaced the slat. She looked up. The Rebbetzin was standing in the doorway.

"I see you're managing nicely," said the Rebbetzin with a kind smile. "The drapes are certainly clean and so are the chairs."

The Rebbetzin walked about, peering closely at these things as she spoke. Sonya stood rooted to her place near the table. She said nothing.

"But no doubt you'll need help with the this," said the Rebbetzin as she came to the table. "I'll stand on your end, and you stand here. There's a loose piece on that side, and I don't want you to hurt yourself."

The Rebbetzin did not notice the flush on Sonya's cheeks. Sonya looked down, and as naturally as she could, changed places with her mistress.

Together they pulled the table apart so that the crack between the leaves could be cleaned. By this time, it was dark outside, and Sonya was dismissed for the day.

After Sonya had gone some distance from the Rabbi's

house, she broke into a run. Twenty minutes later, she arrived breathless at her own doorstep. She had successfully managed to take the pouch home with her, completely undetected. How happily surprised her husband Burik would be!

Yes, Burik was delighted. With glee he poured the sparkling gems upon the table and began to count them. He savored the feel of each stone as it passed through his fingers.

Burik counted one hundred and twenty stones. He leaned back in his chair and smiled with great satisfaction. Burik and Sonya decided that since the theft would surely be discovered it would be best to hide the stones away until the incident was forgotten.

Sonya returned to work as usual the next day. Her mistress greeted her warmly, as she always did. Obviously, thought Sonya, she was still unaware of the missing pouch. The Rebbetzin explained apologetically that although Sonya's services were certainly appreciated it would not be necessary for her to come any more. The holiday would begin the following night, and with Sonya's help the Rebbetzin was just about prepared. Sonya simply smiled and said she understood.

That evening, after Sonya left, the Rebbetzin was relaxed. The house had been thoroughly cleaned, and she was ready to begin cooking in her *Pesachdike* kitchen. Soon her husband and her two sons returned home from *shul* to make *Bedikas Chametz*. The *Bedikah* began, and presently, it reached the table with the secret drawer.

The Rav pulled open the drawer and peered into it. A look of horror spread across his face. He reached deep inside. Nothing. He searched the floor beneath, pulling away the heavy braided rug. Still nothing. The pouch had disappeared.

The Rav and the Rebbetzin were baffled. No one but the family knew of the existence of the secret drawer. It was always kept closed, its treasure reserved for their only daughter's dowry. Only one other person had been aware of the secret. This was Kalman Langsam, the modest young man who had served as personal assistant to the Rav all last year. But Kalman had recently married and moved to Sambor, establishing his own business there.

Perhaps this was just it! argued the sons. From where would a simple man like Kalman have raised enough money to marry, set up a house and invest in his own small business?

The Rav wouldn't hear of such speculation. He knew Kalman as a man of integrity. The Rav went about the house in fierce silence with his candle, wooden spoon and feather, forbidding any further mention of the issue. Even after he finished he purposefully ignored the subject. It was for Hashem to care for finances; it was for him to care for *Pesach.*

Once *Yom Tov* was over, however, the Rav's sons prevailed upon him to visit Kalman. They argued persuasively that Kalman was the logical suspect. Their father would be doing Kalman a kindness by asking him to return the stolen treasure and bringing him to *Teshuvah.*

The Rav set out on his journey with ambivalent feelings. On the one hand, he hoped his sons were not guilty of suspecting an innocent person. On the other hand, the Rav didn't want to believe that the devoted Kalman could betray him so cruelly, overthrowing the base of all Torah ethics with one selfish act of greed. Oh, what a sin he would have brought upon his head!

Kalman greeted the Rav with spontaneous warmth. His sincere joy at seeing his Rav was obvious. The Rav felt relieved. Had Kalman been guilty, he reasoned, this unexpected visit would have come as an unpleasant shock. Still, the Rav felt it necessary to reveal the purpose of his journey and observe Kalman's reaction. He wanted to be certain Kalman was innocent.

In a sad voice, he related the discovery of the missing pouch. He spoke of the bitterness in his sons' hearts, their conviction of Kalman's guilt and how he himself was forced to admit that the facts pointed this way.

"My family insists you have stolen the gems and that it is my obligation to retrieve them from you," he concluded. "After all, it is my daughter's dowry. I argue that the accusation is false and unfair. I only hope that my visit here will establish your innocence in their eyes."

As the Rav spoke, he looked directly into the face of Kalman. Kalman's gaze slowly sank until it fell to the ground. After the Rav finished, Kalman remained silent for a few long minutes. Finally, he raised his eyes and spoke.

"Please grant me forgiveness," he said. "Your sons are wise; they have told you the truth. It is I who stole your savings. I am ashamed. I only hope this will somewhat lessen the real shame I'm bound to feel in the Heavenly Court. I will eventually repay you the full value of the stones, but let me begin by giving you two hundred rubles today. This is all I have on hand. I will send you the rest in separate payments by the end of the year. Only before you go, I entreat you to grant me forgiveness and bless me with strength to endure the hardships I must undergo in this world for my crime."

The Rav was astounded to hear this confession. Disappointment mingled with relief. He shook his head and shrugged his shoulders.

"Because you haven't denied the accusation in any form, I will forgive you without hesitation. Now I can bless your efforts in carrying out the full *Teshuvah* process. You know full well what you must do."

Kalman thanked the Rav for his understanding and escorted him back to the station where they parted in silence. The Rav returned home with his daughter's dowry restored, and the incident was almost forgotten, except for the regular payments arriving from Sambor.

In the meantime, Burik came to the conclusion that the matter had somehow been resolved. There were no concerned policemen hovering about, no distraught neighbors discussing the theft. By now, he felt, it would be safe to spend a small part of the fortune. A celebration would be perfect.

Burik and Sonya invited their closest friends for an informal party. Burik ordered the best whiskey from the local tavern. When the delivery arrived, Burik handed the tavern owner a sparkling gem.

"Go redeem this in the village," he said. "I have found this precious stone in the road and have been assured by the jeweler that it is authentic. Its value is great, greater than my order, but keep the change as a tip."

The tavern owner's eyes lit up when he examined the stone. It was magnificent, and he marvelled at the simple farmer's extravagance.

A week later, he was happily surprised to find the farmer sitting in his tavern. He was in a very good humor and ordered many whiskeys, which he drank in rapid succession. He paid his bill with another glistening stone casually remarking how he had found it in his field.

When Burik returned a third time to the tavern, and offered a third gem to pay his bill, the owner became suspicious. It was possible that the farmer had found one stone on the road. Perhaps even two. But certainly not three. Obviously, some treasure had fallen into Burik's hands. The tavern owner took his suspicions to the local constable.

"The next time this farmer comes into your tavern," advised the constable, "give him enough whiskey to make him drunk. At this point, he can be asked to tell the story of his gems."

Following this suggestion, the tavern owner extracted the desired confession in the presence of friends. Burik admitted that his wife had found the pouch cleverly hidden in the Rav's dining room table and where he had placed it in his own house.

The constable was immediately informed and two guards were issued warrants to search Burik's home for the pouch. They returned within the hour, having successfully uncovered the treasure in its original leather pouch.

The Rav was summoned, and he came with fearful dread and a prayer in his heart. What false accusation would he face? he wondered.

"Are you missing any valuables?" asked the constable, much to the Rav's surprise.

The Rav drew his breath and answered. "I had a treasure of precious stones hidden away in my home. Unfortunately, it was stolen and hasn't been entirely recovered yet."

"How was this treasure kept?" inquired the constable.

"In a leather pouch," the Rav replied.

The officer held this very item up before the Rav.

"Can you identify this as yours?"

"Yes! Yes!" cried the Rav in disbelief.

The constable smiled.

"It is my pleasure to return the gems to their rightful owner," he said.

"But where was this found?" the Rav asked, puzzled.

The constable then told him about Burik and his wife Sonya. The Rav was overjoyed to discover that Kalman was innocent after all and that the original treasure was his again.

Still, the Rav was puzzled by Kalman's behavior. Why had he taken the blame? The Rav packed his bags and traveled to Sambor once more.

Again Kalman greeted his Rav with the greatest honor and warmth. Looking around, the Rav noticed that the house had been emptied of its comfortable furniture. Only a basic table with three or four simple chairs remained.

"I'm sorry," faltered Kalman apologetically, "that I can't offer you to rest on the couch, but perhaps you'll lie down upon the soft bed in my room."

"You have fooled me!" the Rav said as he placed an envelope full of money on the table. "You have sold your furniture to pay me for the treasure you had never even touched! I have since discovered the truth, and my treasure has been returned to me. Only tell me why you admitted to this crime when you were completely innocent? You even took it upon yourself to pay me from your own livelihood and household furnishings. Why?"

Kalman answered quietly, "I discerned from your tone at the time how greatly this loss weighed upon you. You had come all this way because you were so distressed. If I were to deny the theft, you would have returned home still deeply troubled. What would you tell your family? How could you possibly convince them of my innocence? How would your daughter ever marry? The least I could do was to ease your mind."

The Rav listened with great admiration.

"Such self sacrifice is far beyond what the Torah requires of any individual. Because you took the concern of my wealth as your own, may Hashem bless you with great wealth that will be passed on to your children and grandchildren."

This blessing of the Rav was soon fulfilled. Kalman Langsam's business suddenly became unbelievably successful, and his children and grandchildren continue to enjoy his fabulous wealth.

Don Alessandro

Don Alessandro

A S DON ALESSANDRO DE RIVERA'S great coach thundered down the familiar slope with reckless speed, a shrill cry pierced the mountain air. A woman ran into the roadway, waving her hands frantically. It was Isabella, the wife of Pedro the driver and the personal maid of Don Alessandro's wife, Dona Renata.

"Stop! Stop!" she screamed.

The coach came to a sudden jolting halt. The door flew open, and Don Alessandro jumped to the ground.

"Don't go! Don't go!" pleaded the maid, still trembling

violently. "You mustn't go down there."

She pointed down the hill toward the green grassy valley and Don Alessandro's beautiful white villa.

"They've come," she panted breathlessly. "The friars dressed in white. The Inquisition police. They're waiting for you."

Don Alessandro's heart beat wildly as he peered over the hillside and spotted the dreaded white coach behind his stables. Hadn't he prepared himself for this emergency nearly six years ago, in 1492, when King Ferdinand and Queen Isabella announced their Edict of Expulsion? During all these years, Don Alessandro and his family had lived as *marranos*; to the eyes of the world they had adopted the Christian religion, but secretly they remained loyal to their beloved Torah. The fear of discovery hung constantly over their heads. A plan of escape had been devised and well rehearsed, but still Don Alessandro stood in baffled shock as the realization of the actual danger overwhelmed him.

When Don Alessandro had regained his composure, the questions came tumbling out.

"Where are they now? What have they done to Renata? Has Carlos escaped? Where are the rest of the servants? Have they been questioned?"

The maid began to stammer incoherently, but the driver Pedro, her husband, stepped to her side.

"Isabella," he said gently. "Tell us slowly everything that has happened since we've left."

Isabella shook her head.

"You don't understand!" she cried. "There's no time. Soon they will discover I am gone and search for me, thinking I have run away. Dona Renata posted me to wait for you and wave you down before you turned up the road to the villa. Her message was to continue down the road past Salamanca. You must spend *Pesach* in hiding because you are under Inquisitional suspicion, and the villa will be under surveillance until you are found and arrested. I must go now," she said looking back over her shoulder. "There is already a policeman looking for me in the yard. I must return immediately."

The maid stooped low and scrambled through a hedge. A moment later she was bounding down the grassy hillside.

"But wait!" called Pedro running after his wife.

Isabella turned around for an instant and motioned him to stop. Then she continued down and slipped quietly behind the porch. She picked up the broom that she had purposely placed there before. The guard had just surveyed the yard from the opposite direction and now turned around to find her holding the broom.

"So there you are!" he said with an evil laugh. "Why have you been hiding from me?"

Isabella coldly turned around.

"Excuse me, Senor Cabezas," she said. "My mistress has asked me to sweep this path, and you are standing in my way."

Senor Cabezas frowned and stalked off.

Pedro observed all this from his position on the hillside. He was relieved to see the policeman walk away as his wife calmly resumed her work. Don Alessandro was already waiting in the driver's seat of the coach, with the horse reins in his hands.

"Pedro," he called as his servant raised himself up and turned around. "Remain here with your wife. You can steal your way into the house. Hide yourself in one of the secret chambers in the cellar. If you are discovered, explain that you are an ill servant who has been kept in confinement for fear of spreading your disease."

As Don Alessandro spoke, Pedro stood on the ground, mixed feelings playing across his face. At first he was ready to follow this plan and return to his wife and her mistress at the villa. But when he looked up at Don Alessandro's pale face and twitching features, he realized his place was at his master's side. Don Alessandro sensed his hesitation.

"The women will need a man to whom they can turn at any moment," he continued. "It is true that the women are well prepared to follow the escape route if, Heaven forbid, it is necessary for them to run. But they will still need a man's strength to fend for their survival."

"But you forget about your own son Carlos. He is strong and courageous. And nearly seventeen. What better protection could I offer?"

"He is only a child!" Don Alessandro cried.

"You need me more," said Pedro.

"What do you mean?" asked Don Alessandro sharply.

"It is painful for my master to admit that his health has been failing him," said Pedro in a humble tone. "Especially after the expulsion, the responsibility of all our lives has brought tension and physical strain on his health. His heart beats rapidly and even as he sits this very minute, the horse reins in his hands shake uncontrollably. It is impossible for him to travel alone, especially under such difficult circumstances. I would never be able to forgive myself for abandoning my master at this most desperate hour."

Don Alessandro drew a long sigh and looked down at the road below him.

"This is the very reason I ask you to remain here," he said. "Perhaps you don't realize just how dangerous it will be for you to be found with me. For if, Heaven forbid, I am arrested, you are bound to share my fate. This will endanger Isabella as well. You have no right to speak for her life."

"On the contrary," Pedro said as he hoisted himself up beside his master, easily taking the reins from his hands. "In the event you are caught, Heaven forbid, I promise to detach myself from you and return here. I will warn the family of your peril and help them escape before the Inquisition grabs them up in its iron fingers. In any case, we had better move on before we are spotted right here. May I recommend that you sit inside the coach so that you aren't immediately recognized?"

Don Alessandro followed this advice mechanically. He plunged wearily onto the velvet cushioned seat inside and leaned back as the blood drained from his head. He felt a sudden release of the tight pressure that had built up inside his forehead and temples, and his facial muscles relaxed. Don Alessandro closed his eyes as the carriage rumbled down the mountain, pulling him further away from his beloved ones with every gallop.

How he had anticipated this homecoming just minutes ago. He'd been away on business for three long months. It had been a most trying period. The Spaniards spoke of nothing but the capture of heretics for which the Inquisition awarded huge prizes. The past four weeks every acquaintance mentioned the next *auto-da-fe* in Salamnca, scheduled for the first day of *Pesach*. What a spectacle it would be! Rumor had it that the Inquisition had already sentenced nine Jewish heretics to be burned publicly at the stake. The capture of the tenth was to be a grand surprise for many of the citizens of Salamanca who were familiar with the heretic and respected him as a wealthy and devout Christian. Every business associate promised to meet with him at the "Holiday Fireworks," since Don Alessandro lived on the outskirts of Salamanca and would surely attend this fantastic spectacle. Surely, no true Spaniard would miss it.

Don Alessandro had felt uneasy as the heavy hands had slapped his back and the vulgar laughter filled his ears. Perhaps he'd like to place a bet on the identity of this tenth heretic? they had asked. When he did not join in their merriment a sudden coldness surrounded him as his Christian associates squinted into his face. Perhaps, here at their very sides stood another heretic.

The only solace Don Alessandro had found in this business venture was his financial success. His plan was to earn just enough money to afford him a private ship. He'd hire it to transport his wife and youngest son Carlos with all their possessions to the Netherlands. The rest of Don Alessandro's children anxiously awaited their arrival there. They themselves were all married, raising families of their own, free from religious persecution. Once in Amsterdam they could return to living as Jews in the open. Alessandro,

Renata, Carlos, Pedro and Isabella could once again become Yitzchak, Renah, Chaim, Pinchas and Rivkah.

Don Alessandro had been able to raise the bulk of the necessary funds over the past twelve weeks. If he could only hold out till after *Pesach!* As he travelled home, he had pictured himself greeting Renata on the lovely veranda, telling her the happy news. What a joyous *Pesach* would follow, with the taste of freedom upon their very lips.

Such were Don Alessandro's thoughts as he had urged Pedro on, the carriage swiftly flying down the road toward the villa. His excitement had mounted with the momentum of the horse's gallop as they drew ever closer to home. But suddenly every bright hope was turned into dark dread, without as much as Renata's comforting voice. Would he ever see her face again? What would become of Carlos?

A tear welled up in each of Don Alessandro's eyes as the uncertainty of the future loomed like an evil black shadow before him. But he must not despair! Had he truly abandoned his deep Jewish faith instilled by his own father and inspired by the hundreds of ancestors before him? He must have hope, faith, trust and belief in the mercy of the *Ribono Shel Olam.* Many times he had given Renata courage with the word *bitachon,* and she in turn had pulled him out of many dark moments with that very word. Don Alessandro dared not carry a *Siddur* in his pocket, but he closed his eyes and prayed from memory with deep feelings. He repeated the *Sh'ma* several times until he fell asleep, as the carriage rolled on and on.

All this while, Pedro drove with tensed strength. He sat on the edge of his seat, the reins tightly clutched in his hands. He squinted through the darkness at the overgrown roadside, until finally his back ached and his whole body was overstrained. If he did not stop to rest, he thought, it would be impossible for him to drive in the morning. Pedro pulled the coach to the edge of a wooded hill. In the distance, a small village could be discerned by the lanterns twinkling through its windows. How snug and friendly these quaint Spanish hamlets appeared, Pedro reflected. But how cruel were its bloodthirsty inhabitants! Any Spaniard would be only too happy to deliver them into the hands of the Inquisition. Pedro leaned back on his seat, drawing his cloak tightly about him. He closed his eyes with a prayer for the protection of the *Ribono Shel Olam.*

The gray dawn filtered through the windows of the coach, and Don Alessandro awoke with a shiver. For a moment he could not imagine why he had spent the night in his carriage. Surely he could afford a room at a hotel, or at least a roadside inn. He was accustomed to sleeping in great luxurious beds under soft, warm blankets. Just the night before he had shared a room with Pedro at the prestigious Las Palomas, only a day's ride from his villa.

Don Alessandro sat bolt upright as the events of yesterday flooded back to him. He opened the carriage door and was greeted by a chilly blast of air. The first thing Don Alessandro noticed was a small brook winding its way through the great knotted trees only a few paces away. Immediately, Don Alessandro went to wash his hands in its icy waters. Next, he gently awakened Pedro who lay across his seat bundled in his wool cloak.

"Come sleep inside the carriage," he said softly. "There's no reason for you to catch cold up here."

Pedro yawned and followed like a child. Don Alessandro opened the door and helped him settle comfortably on the seat.

"I'm going to *daven Shacharis* now," he said. "And then I will take a little walk. Rest until I come back."

Pedro had hardly even heard as he drifted off to sleep.

Refreshed by the invigorating spring air, Don Alessandro took his *Tallis, Tefillin* and a *Siddur* from a secret compartment in the carriage and went into the woods. Each word he uttered took on new dimensions in these peaceful surroundings. Don Alessandro concluded his prayer with thoughts of eternal redemption for all Jews in Yerushalayim and then closed his *Siddur* with a kiss.

Redemption. . . Deliverance. . . *Pesach.* The festival of freedom would start this evening. Don Alessandro sighed. How would they celebrate the *Seder?* What would they eat? Perhaps something grew here in the woods. But no. Spring had just arrived, and the tree branches were still bare. As Don Alessandro's gaze scanned the great trees up and down, his eye came to rest on a squirrel perched in the hollow of a huge oak. It held a nut in its hands, while its teeth pecked at it several times. Don Alessandro stood very still, watching as the squirrel cracked the nut open and chewed out its meat. This accomplished the shells fell to the ground and Don Alessandro observed the squirrel darting into the hollow for a second nut.

Stealthily, Don Alessandro approached the next oak tree and bent down to examine its hollow. Sure enough, there too lay a treasure of nuts. Don Alessandro reached into the hole and quickly filled his pockets. He returned to the coach.

"It's *Pesach* tonight, and I've collected a delicacy for our *Seder*," he told Pedro who was now awake.

"And just where will we make our *Seder?*" Pedro asked dismally.

Don Alessandro made no reply, and Pedro took the opportunity to state his preference, as he rubbed his sore back.

"Rather than spending another night in the coach, perhaps we should dignify the *Yom Tov* and sleep upon some straw in a hayloft. We can cover ourselves with more straw and crack the nuts under its cover. Certainly no one will discover us."

"That's if the animals don't," Don Alessandro smiled wryly, hardly relishing the thought of spending the night in a barn. "Why shouldn't we ride into the next city and look for decent accomodations? As long as I keep myself concealed in the carriage no one will recognize us. As a matter of fact, we can break off the insignia that identifies the coach as my property. We can even look for some fresh fruit in the marketplace before *Yom Tov.*"

Pedro was reluctant to accept this plan.

"You forget that you are my responsibility," he said. "By moving through a city the chances of capture will be increased tenfold. Why should we risk it? However, I will gladly follow your suggestion about the insignia."

He picked up a heavy jagged rock that lay at their feet, raised it high above his head and brought it crashing down on the metal emblem protruding from the rear of the coach. Instantly, the emblem broke off. Pedro picked it up from the dust and flung it far out into the woods.

"Let them find us there!" he said as he clapped the dust off his hands with finality.

Don Alessandro smiled, but his mind was still on the next city.

"There's no reason," he argued, "that we must do with so little for *Yom Tov* when I have so much money right here. Are we so cowardly? Do we have so little faith as to shy away from decent fare and lodging in honor of *Yom Tov*? When we reach the next city road, I insist we follow it, at least till the marketplace. I will remain hidden in the coach, and you will go about making the necessary purchases."

They rode only a short distance before coming to the market town of Esplanada. The marketplace was crowded with sellers and buyers. There were meats of every variety, as well as fish, fowl and hundreds of species of fruits and vegetables. There were even plants for sale. Beads, linens, tools and clothing overflowed from the stalls. Furniture and horses were auctioned off every hour from large platforms.

Pedro walked among the fruit stands, searching out exotic varieties in honor of *Yom Tov*. He dared not be seen near the vegetables. Everywhere he turned a monk or friar stood in the aisle. They were certainly aware that *Pesach* was this evening, and they would be watching for anyone buying *marror*, the bitter herb. It was available just across the aisle, though Pedro pretended not to notice it.

Pedro's quick eye fell upon a carefully wrapped package

that was suddenly knocked from under the arm of a distinguished looking gentleman. A monk standing next to him quickly bent to retrieve it, but the gentleman was faster, much faster.

"Excuse me," he said to the monk as they both scrambled for it. "I got it myself, but thank you anyway."

The gentleman held on to the package as dearly as to his own life. Pedro watched the gentleman from behind, somehow certain that the bag contained *marror*.

The gentleman weaved through the crowd, Pedro following close behind, until he came to a quiet, secluded street. The gentleman mopped his brow and sighed with relief. He continued to walk until he came to the largest home on the street. He climbed up the porch and rang the bell in a series of musical peals that must have been a passing signal. Instantly, a maid opened the door, and the gentleman thrust the package, like a bundle of hot coals, into her hands.

The gentleman disappeared into the house, and Pedro detached himself from the shadows of the tree under which he was hiding and returned to Don Alessandro. Pedro told him all he had seen in the marketplace and that it was likely this gentleman was a *marrano*.

"Do you remember the way to his home?" asked Don Alessandro with growing excitement.

Pedro nodded.

"Then let us go," said Don Alessandro with little reservation.

"Perhaps we ought to exercise caution," Pedro suggested. "How do we know who this man really is? He may have been set-up by the Inquisition to attract and fool Jewish onlookers like ourselves."

"That is highly unlikely," remarked Don Alessandro. "You personally observed his behavior even when he thought no one was watching."

Pedro bowed to his master's logic. Once more he climbed up to his seat, took the reins in his hands and headed for the

110

gentleman's home. Don Alessandro waited in the coach while Pedro rang the musical bell. Presently it was answered by another maid.

"I have come to see the master of the house," Pedro said in his most authorative tone.

"What is your name, *senor?*" the maid inquired.

"Tell him," said Pedro, reassuming his deep tone, "that his desperate brother has come for his aid."

The maid looked at him curiously and went off to deliver this strange message. Shortly, she returned with the gentleman.

"What can I do for you, *senor?*" He asked politely.

"May I speak with you in private?" Pedro asked.

"I'm afraid I do not recognize you. How are you my brother?"

"Oh, in many ways, in many ways," Pedro said wistfully.

The gentleman clapped his hands and a valet appeared.

"Search this man," he said to the valet. "If he is unarmed, accompany him to my office where I shall wait."

The gentleman went down a long corridor, his footsteps drained as the thorough search began. Finally, he was permitted private entrance into the gentleman's plush office. It was furnished much in the same style as his own master's. Pedro looked at the bookcase against the wall and wondered if it too covered a secret sliding panel covering *sefarim* concealed within the very walls.

"What do you see?" the gentleman asked Pedro, growing nervous. "Which book on my shelves interests you so greatly?"

"The one on exotic vegetables," Pedro answered. "Bitter herbs, in particular."

"I am puzzled," said the gentleman, rising from behind his desk and removing his spectacles. "I have no such books. I neither know you as a brother, nor am I a botanist. You must have mistaken my identity with that of someone else."

"Perhaps," Pedro continued, undaunted. "You have a *haggadah?*"

"I do not know what you are talking about!" the gentleman said obviously disturbed.

Now Pedro was certain his host was a *marrano.*

"Very well," said Pedro. "You have convinced me that I can trust you with my secret. I will play no more games to frighten you. My reference is to the *marror* you have purchased in the marketplace today. Obviously, you remain a true Jew. I am proud to admit that I too am a *marrano.*"

The gentleman was aghast. He trembled visibly, unsure of Pedro's sincerity.

"Let me reassure you," said Pedro in his soothing way, "and prove that we are indeed brothers. My master is Don Alessandro de Rivera of Salamanca, a distinguised *marrano.* His grown children left Spain in 1492, when the expulsion was first announced. But he and his wife, along with their youngest son, remained behind to care for his aged and ailing parents who couldn't possibly have survived the journey. Eventually, Don Alessandro's father passed away, and in a matter of weeks, his mother followed. Ever since, Don Alessandro has been planning his own escape from Spain. But now the Inquisition is after him, and so he left his family for *Pesach*, to go into hiding. He is waiting this very minute in his coach just outside your door."

The gentleman dropped down in the chair behind his desk, holding his head in his hands. Had he been discovered, after all? Could he dare believe this man spoke the truth? The name Don Alessandro de Rivera was familiar to him, in two connections. First, he had had a childhood friend by that name. But more recently, the name Don Alessandro was on the lips of friars and monks everywhere he went. This heretic was to be the main attraction of the "Holiday Fireworks" in Salamanca the following day, but this Don Alessandro was elusive. He had managed to evade the Inquisitional police.

"Where did Don Alessandro grow up?" the gentleman asked in a tremulous voice.

"In Seville," said Pedro anxiously.

The gentleman sighed with relief. But still this could be a trap, a ploy of familiar names. Perhaps his loyalties to the church were being tested. The gentleman would make no verbal admission of his Jewish belief until he were completely convinced of the truth of this servant's story.

"Bring in your master, then," he said, hoping to establish the truth. Maybe he would recognize Don Alessandro as the friend of his youth. When Don Alessandro was searched and brought to the office, the gentleman lifted his hands in delight.

"So it is indeed you, Don Alessandro!" he cried. "I recognize your face."

"And it is you, Don Alfonso Ballesteros," cried Don Alessandro with equal joy. "My good friend Shimeon! It has been so many years!"

"Do you realize you are a high stake for the Inquisition?" asked Don Alfonso. "They are after your blood like thirsty dogs. They expect to burn you at tomorrow's *auto-da-fe*, and collect great rewards from your estate."

Don Alessandro shivered and his face paled. Would his wife escape in time?

"But fear not," Don Alfonso added quickly, grabbing hold of Don Alessandro's arm. "I will hide you well. You will celebrate the *Seder* tonight here with my family in our hidden cellar chambers."

"I cannot do that," said Don Alessandro withdrawing from Don Alfonso's grasp. "It is enough that I endanger the life of my loyal servant Pedro, but I cannot, Heaven forbid, have the blood of your family on my head as well. What if I am discovered here?"

"Heaven forbid!" cried Don Alfonso. "If that be the case, it will be on my account, not yours. For if the police come here, it is to arrest me, not you. You will only be a great bonus. I insist you celebrate *Pesach* properly, with my family."

Don Alessandro bowed graciously, and the arrangements were made.

The three men, together with two of Alfonso's own sons,

davened in a hidden cellar chamber reached through an ingeniously concealed trap door in the cellar floor. In an adjoining chamber the *Seder* table was set up, adorned with the special *Pesach* foods. Many had been acquired months in advance and carefully stored away for this night. The *matzos* had been stored away from the previous year, and though a bit stale, they were still genuine *shmurah matzos*.

After *Maariv*, everyone took their seats around the *Seder* table. Don Alfonso, dressed in his white *kittel*, remarked on the kindness of the *Ribono Shel Olam*. Here he had every conceivable *Pesach* need at hand during this black hour of persecution. His entire family surrounded him, and he even had the good fortune to have guests at his table. Here they sat in a cellar beneath a cellar, deep within the earth, and yet they felt like kings on their thrones.

At this moment, Don Alessandro missed his family terribly. He wondered if they had been able to make a *Seder*, or if, Heaven forbid, they languished as prisoners of the Inquisition on this night of freedom. He shuddered. How gladly he'd give his life to save his family from those horrible tortures. Don Alfonso looked at him, perceiving his anxiety.

"Tonight the *Ribono Shel Olam* protects his people," said Don Alfonso with conviction. "We even leave our doors unlocked —"

Indeed, the door two flights up had been left unlocked. The faint vibrations of its opening and closing were felt with dread in the deep cellar. Don Alessandro froze in his seat as the adrenalin raced through his body causing his heart to pound loudly in his chest. Only his eyes remained mobile, and they riveted themselves upon Pedro.

Run, Pedro, run! his mind was screaming. Did you forget your promise? But no voice came into his throat.

The sound of heavy footsteps came closer and closer. The trap door creaked open and a single pair of boots descended the ladder.

He's only one, and we are nine, thought Don Alessandro

with growing desperation. Why don't we pounce upon him and kill him? His mind spun in a wild frenzy, but the others simply watched the man in the white Inquisitional robe continue down the ladder. Have they gone mad? thought Don Alessandro.

"Kill the friar!" he shouted, finally pulling himself up with extraordinary effort and finding his voice. Don Alfonso and one of his sons grabbed Don Alessandro's arms.

"You're all traitors," cried Pedro, rising from his own seat. "This was a trap. A trap!"

"No, it is not a trap," said Don Alfonso quietly, shaking his head. "This is my wife's brother Miguel who is also a *marrano*."

The friar threw off his hood and untied his robe, revealing a white *yarmulka* and *kittel*.

"I have come to join your *Seder*," he said calmly. "Have I missed *kiddush*?"

Don Alfonso's family burst into laughter as the tension broke, but Don Alessandro and Pedro still sat in subdued amazement. Don Alfonso spoke softly to them, explaining how his brother pretended so well to be a devout Christian he had been appointed a high Inquisition official. His position had enabled him to arrange for strange disappearances of suspected *marranos* before they were arrested and tried.

"Have you calmed yourselves enough so that we may begin the *Seder*?" asked Don Alfonso kindly as he finished his explanation.

Don Alessandro and Pedro both nodded.

"Excuse me, Alfonso," intervened Miguel, "but I think it only fair that you introduce your guests to me now."

As soon as he had heard Don Alessandro's name, Miguel's eyes opened wide.

"You are Don Alessandro de Rivera of Salamanca?" he questioned.

"Yes."

"Then perhaps we shall have to delay the *Seder* for a

while. I have some unfortunate news for you. Tomorrow, a great *auto-da-fe* is scheduled for Salamanca. You were to be the main attraction because of your fine reputation as a noble Christian and a wealthy businessman. Your house is under Inquisitional watch, and early tomorrow morning your family will be seized by the police. They expect you to surrender yourself in exchange for their freedom, though we know well that once the Inquisition has made prisoners of any Jews they are only released in the form of ashes."

Don Alessandro's heart sickened at these words. Miguel continued.

"But do not despair, Don Alessandro. I will ride to your villa right now and arrest your family in the name of the Inquisition. I will bring them here. Immediately after *Yom Tov*, you will all disguise yourselves as beggars, and I will arrange for passage on a small ship bound for the Netherlands where you can be reunited with the rest of your family. All your possessions must of course be left behind. Your villa and all of its contents will fall into the greedy hands of the Inquisition. But you and your family will be alive and free to serve the *Ribono Shel Olam* as you please. That is the most important thing."

"I shall be eternally grateful to you, Don Miguel," Don Alessandro said, overwhelmed by Miguel's generosity, "but my villa is very far from here. How can you get there and come back in time? It took us nearly six hours to get here."

"That is because you traveled along the back roads to avoid the police. I can take the swiftest horses and travel through the open city highways. I can go there and return in a matter of three hours. Is it fair to delay the *Seder* that long?" Miguel wondered aloud.

"Go this very minute, without as much as another thought," said Don Alfonso with urgency in his voice. "It is a matter of *Pikuach Nefesh*, saving Jewish lives."

Miguel had already risen and was draping his Inquisitional robes over his shoulders.

"Wait," said Don Alessandro. "My wife and the others will

run when they see you at the door. We have worked out an elaborate plan of escape, and I am afraid they will waste precious time."

"Maybe there is a password to be used in the event of such an emergency?" suggested Miguel.

"No, I'm afraid not," said Don Alessandro thoughtfully. "Although perhaps we should have had one. But we spoke very often about the word *bitachon*, trust in the *Ribono Shel Olam*. As soon as the door is opened say you have a message from me, and it is to have *bitachon*. She will understand."

Miguel climbed up the ladder to the trap door.

"Give me about three hours," he said as he disappeared from sight.

"May the *Ribono Shel Olam* be with you," came the cry from every side.

As soon as he was gone Don Alessandro and Pedro retreated to a corner where they said *Tehillim* together. Don Alfonso and his sons sat at the table discussing the wonders of *Pesach*, while the women set extra places at the table for their anticipated guests.

Four hours went by. Don Alfonso suggested they begin the *Seder*. Miguel could make *kiddush* for Don Alessandro's family when they arrived. Alfonso filled his silver goblet with wine and raised it in his right hand. His voice rang out with great emotion as he recited the *kiddush* for this holiday of deliverance. Don Alessandro held up his goblet and summoned the strength of faith into his voice.

"Wait a moment!" a muffled familiar voice called from above. "Just wait a moment!"

Don Alessandro's heart raced with joy as the sounds of many footsteps clambering down from cellar to cellar grew louder and louder.

"Welcome, welcome," said Don Alfonso as the dusty travelers settled themselves around the table.

"Are we in time for *kiddush*?" Miguel asked breathlessly, as if he had never gone. He was still panting hard.

Warmth and light filled the hidden cellar as the Ballesteros and de Rivera families lost themselves in the beauty of the *Pesach Seder.*

One after the other, they stood up and in ringing voices pronounced the holy words of the *kiddush,* thanking the *Ribbono Shel Olam* for choosing them from among all the other peoples of the world and sanctifying them with His *mitzvos.*

The *Seder* continued far, far into the night. The stories of the oppression in Egypt thousands of years ago brought sympathetic tears to the eyes of the indomitable people huddled in the Spanish cellar.

As the *Seder* drew to a close, Don Alfonso rose to his feet. His eyes shone with the fire that burned in his heart.

"Come, my friends, let us dance!" he exclaimed. "Le'-shanah Haba'ah Bi'yerushalayim! Next year in Yerushalayim."

A Friend in Need

A Friend in Need
THE STORY OF NOAM SHABBOS

A FTER SUFFERING through ten years of banishment to Siberia, a Russian family emigrated to Eretz Yisrael and settled in the Holy City. Several of the family members were ill and required constant warmth. Noam Shabbos found them a well-heated apartment and undertook its upkeep.

A YOUNG MAN was spotted buying chicken legs in a butcher store before Shabbos. It seemed the young man never had enough money for any-

חברת "נועם שבת"
מחלקת משלוחים לנצרכים
רחוב עזרא 18, בעיה"ק ירושלם.
ת"ד 5354, טל' 822835

thing else. Noam Shabbos arranged for the butcher to give the young man chickens every week — on its account.

TRIPLETS WERE BORN to an impoverished family in the Holy City. The parents were too sick with worry to be gladdened by the joy of new life. Where would they get enough cribs, diapers and baby clothing? How would they care for the infants without a mother's helper? The compassionate assistance of Noam Shabbos made the arrival of the triplets a truly joyous occasion.

A FATHER OF SEVEN CHILDREN suffered a serious heart attack. The mother could not leave her little children to take a job. There was no food in the house, no money for clothing and other basic necessities. Noam Shabbos stepped in and provided for the family until the father recovered and was able to return to his job.

FIRE DESTROYED the home of a family of modest means. The father wouldn't hear of accepting charity and moved his entire family into a one-room apartment. Noam Shabbos heard of their plight and began delivering food packages to their door in the middle of the night.

*   *   *

There are thousands of similar Noam Shabbos stories in the Holy City of Yerushalayim. Noam Shabbos distributes weekly food packages to over one hundred needy families before every Shabbos at a cost of over $10,000 per month. In the months of Nissan and Tishrei, Noam Shabbos also distrib-

utes wine, fish, meat and matzos to over 1,200 families who cannot manage the additional Yom Tov expenses from their own meager resources, bringing the costs up to $60,000 per month.

Noam Shabbos also operates . . .

. . . a wholesale food emporium where large families too proud to accept charity can buy food at giveaway prices.

. . . a periodic distribution of thousands of pairs of shoes to needy families.

. . . a hospitality center offering temporary sleeping quarters for the homeless.

. . . an open kitchen where the hungry can always find a hot meal.

. . . a twice yearly clothing and household goods distribution program, including blankets, pillows and assorted housewares.

. . . a free loan fund.

*　　*　　*

Whether it is feeding the hungry, clothing the poor or just lending a sympathetic ear to a person in distress the people of Yerushalayim know that Noam Shabbos is a friend that is always there.

Glossary of Terms

(Terms are in Hebrew unless otherwise indicated.)

afikomen: portion of *matzoh* traditionally hidden during the *Seder*

auto-da-fe: burning at the stake [Portugese

Bais Medrash: house of study

Baruch Hashem: blessed is the Name

Bedikas Chametz: search for *chametz*

bitachon: trust

Bruchim Habaim: blessed are those who come, welcome

chametz: leaven

charossess: special *Seder* condiment

cherus: freedom

daven: pray [Yiddish]

Erev Pesach: the day before *Pesach*

Erev Shabbos: the day before *Shabbos*

G'mara: Talmud

goyim: gentiles

Gut Yom Tov: happy holiday [Yiddish]

Hachnasas Orchim: hospitality

Hagaddah: Seder liturgy

Hallel: songs of praise

Hamotzi: blessing over bread

Hashem: G-d, the Name

hatzlachah: success

Havdalah: ritual marking the end of *Shabbos* or *Yom Tov*

kashering: making kosher

Kehillah: community

kiddush: sanctification

Kiddush Hashem: sanctification of the Name

kittel: special white robe worn during *Seder* [Yiddish]

Lael Shimurim: protected night

Le'shanah Haba'ah Bi'yerushalayim: next year in Jerusalem

Maariv: evening prayer

Mah Nishtanah: "How is it different?", Four Questions traditionally asked by children during the *Seder*

marrano: secret Jew [Spanish]

marror: bitter herbs used during *Seder*

matzoh: unleavened bread

mazel: fortune, luck

menuchah: serenity

mezuzah: scroll attached to the doorpost

Minchah: afternoon prayer

minyan: quorum of ten for prayer

Mitzrayim: Egypt

mitzvah: commandment

Oy: interjection [Yiddish]

Pesach: festival of Passover

Pesachdike: special for *Pesach* [Yiddish]

Pikuach Nefesh: mortal danger

Purim: festival of Lots

pushka: charity box [Yiddish]

Rabbosai: gentlemen

Rav: rabbi

Ribono Shel Olam: Master of the Universe

Seder: elaborately ceremonial *Pesach* feast

sefarim: books

senor: sir [Spanish]

seudah: festive meal

Shabbos: Sabbath

Shacharis: morning prayer

Shalom Aleichem: peace to you, greeting

shmurah matzoh: specially supervised *matzoh*

shul: synagogue [Yiddish]

Siddur: prayer book

Sukkos: festival of Tabernacles

sou: old French coin [French]

Tallis: prayer shawl

Teffilin: phylacteries

Tehillim: Book of Psalms

Teshuvah: repentance

traifah: non-kosher

tzedakah: charity

Viduy: confession of sins

yarmulka: skullcap [Yiddish]

Yiddishkeit: Jewishness [Yiddish]

Yom Tov: festival